Mac MacDonnell had come in.

She had entered from the shower room and was in front of her locker by the time I became aware of her. She was naked and utterly uncaring about it. She had small breasts and slim thighs and muscles of proud power that wreathed her arms and legs — the physique of an athlete that performed beyond pain or earthly distraction.

I noticed. She had a body that made me want to take my clothes off. Under the circumstances, it was only a passing thought.

Mac spoke before I could. "Stay clear, O'Neill. Just stay the fuck away."

Blue Diamonds' Coach DeeDee Lefevre appeared at her office door. "O'Neill," she said, "don't you think you ought to check in with the coach before you make yourself at home?"

It seemed as good a way as any to bail out. "Sure," I said.

Smokey O

A ROMANCE BY

CELIA COHEN

The Naiad Press, Inc.
1994

Printed in the United States of America on acid-free paper
First Edition

Edited by Christine Cassidy
Cover design by Pat Tong and Bonnie Liss
    (Phoenix Graphics)
Typeset by Sandi Stancil

Library of Congress Cataloging-in-Publication Data

Cohen, Celia, 1953–
    Smokey O / by Celia Cohen.
        p.   cm.
    ISBN 1-56280-057-4
    1. Women baseball players—United States—Ficiton. 2.
Lesbians—United States—Fiction.   I. Title.
PS3553.04188S63   1994
813'.54—dc20
                                                      93-41792
                                                      CIP

For Mary, Robbie, John, Joyce
and especially my sister,
who put on their rally caps for me
when I needed them most.

About the Author

Celia Cohen is a newspaper writer. She lives in Delaware with Joyce, and their dog Zippy, whose name is entirely the author's fault.

CHAPTER ONE

"Yo, Smokey," the Boston sportswriter called to me. "How do you feel?"

"Like a Christian who's been traded to the lions," I said.

The sportswriter laughed, flipping open her notebook to find a clean page. She had her story for the day, and she knew it.

"I'm going to miss you, Smokey," she said. "You always give good quote."

* * * * *

That's me, all right. Smokey O'Neill, known to the space-conscious headline writers as Smokey O.

Until that morning, I was the first base player for the Boston Colonials of the Women's Baseball League. Then Coach Pettibone summoned me to her office and announced with vicious glee that she had traded me to the Delaware Blue Diamonds.

"I don't mind telling you," she said, shredding a cigarette and compulsively shaping the little brown pile of tobacco that lay on her otherwise empty desk, "that this is one of the happiest days of my life."

I didn't have far to go to join my new club. The Boston Colonials were in Newark, Delaware, to play the Blue Diamonds. All I had to do was walk down the corridors of Du Pont Stadium from the visitors' clubhouse to the home team's. That's when I passed the Boston sportswriter.

Like a Christian who's been traded to the lions. I wasn't kidding.

The Boston Colonials and the Delaware Blue Diamonds were battling for first place in the Eastern Division of the W.B.L., the Women's Baseball League. It was a rivalry that was getting as serious as the Yankees and the Dodgers.

For the first three years of the league, the Delaware Blue Diamonds had won the division and gone on to beat the winner of the Western Division for the W.B.L. Crown. Then, for the first time last year, the Blue Diamonds were dethroned in the East by the Boston Colonials, who proceeded to blow the championship series.

That was my first year of pro ball.

On the day I was traded, Boston was in first place and threatening to stomp the Blue Diamonds.

The two teams were playing a three-game series, and Boston had won the first game.

There had been a little animosity, though. You might say I was the cause of it.

The heart of the Delaware Blue Diamonds was Jill MacDonnell, Mac for short, a lanky center fielder with dark hair and dark eyes and a stare that could melt ice cubes.

Mac was more than the heart of the Blue Diamonds. She was practically the heart of the entire Women's Baseball League.

Mac had been an American hero for a decade, ever since the Russians conned the Olympics committee into making women's baseball an event. American women were still playing softball then, not baseball, and it was tough to put a team together. Mac was the center fielder on her college softball team, playing in her senior year, and she volunteered.

The Olympics were held in Atlanta that year. The U.S. women, many of them veterans of sandlot games and Little League, had baseball in their blood, the way all Americans seem to, regardless of gender, race, creed or criminal record. From the time you're a tot, you seem to grow up knowing how to pound your glove and spit, and kids learn the mantra, "You can't get out on a foul," quicker than they learn, "Honor thy father and thy mother."

There was a lot of pressure on the American women's team, but they played as though they were born to win — and no one played better than Jill MacDonnell.

Mac played with an American haughtiness, making her someone to admire, if not to approach.

When she wasn't hitting game-winning RBIs from the cleanup spot, she was whipping balls in from center field and cutting down runners on their way to a sure triple. She was fast and she was strong, and the U.S. team was riding on luck and laughter under her lead. They just slaughtered the other teams — until they came to the Russians.

The Russians played with all the grace of robots, but they could play. It would have been funny, watching them imitate American idiosyncracies like high-fives, except that they were grimly efficient. People had the willies at home, afraid that the Russians were going to beat us at the Great American Pastime.

I know. I was watching. I was twelve at the time.

Mom and apple pie were at stake when the U.S. took the field, our team in blue uniforms and theirs in red. The Russians hung in as fiercely as a Siberian winter. Our team threw good leather at them but weak bats, and going into the bottom of the ninth, the U.S. women trailed 3–0.

America hung its head. It covered its eyes. It went to the refrigerator for something to eat, anything to stave off the all-but-certain humiliation unfolding wherever there was a television set. A baseball game, to be ended with the playing of the Russian national anthem!

The first American batter walked, but the second one struck out. The third laid down a nifty little drag bunt that put runners on first and second. A double steal on the next pitch put them on second and third, but the batter popped out. Two down.

A cheap infield single loaded the bases, and then

Mac MacDonnell sauntered to the plate as cool as a kid on the first day of summer. America held its breath and waited as she kicked at the dirt in the batter's box and scanned the pitcher with that dark laser stare.

She didn't make America wait long. With a hitch of her slim shoulders, she took the first pitch downtown, for one of the greatest grand slams in American history. It was one of those immortal sports moments: Babe Ruth pointing to the stands, a weeping Michael Chang falling onto the soft red clay of the tennis court at the French Open, Mac MacDonnell hitting an in-your-face home run against the Russians.

The game ended with the score at 4–3 in the worst Russian meltdown since Chernobyl.

There was no place for Mac to showcase the talent at home. She did a round of charity commercials for the Special Olympics, but she hated interviews and refused to do endorsements. She took her college diploma and got a job at a bank.

But America came calling four years later for the next Olympics. Mac, who had been playing some softball, said yes and carried the flag in the parade of Olympians.

Expectations were high, but Mac wasn't the same wonder that she had been in Atlanta. Her hitting was respectable but not outstanding, and every game seemed to produce a new American star.

But the script was the same. The game for the gold medal pitted the U.S. women against the Russians in a rematch.

Mac couldn't do anything right. She struck out twice with runners in scoring position, and the

Americans went into the ninth inning nursing a 1–0 lead, with the Russians batting last.

There were two quick outs and then a double. And then the next Russian hit a grounder that just skidded past the second base player and into the outfield. It should have been a run-scoring single to tie the game, but somehow Mac had sensed it coming and skipped in from center field to back up the play.

She scooped up the ball and rifled it to the catcher, who was almost too astonished to glove it. In the bone-crunching collision at home plate, the Russian runner was out, the Americans had another gold medal, and Mac was a hero again.

She went back to the bank, but not for long. This time some promoter realized that women's baseball was exciting. It could make money. Two years later, the Women's Baseball League — with twelve teams split evenly between the Eastern Division and the Western Division — was formed.

Delaware, being the first state, got the first pick in the draft. The Blue Diamonds would have been the laughingstock of the civilized world if they hadn't chosen Jill MacDonnell.

Mac carried that team in its early seasons the way she had carried the U.S. women in the first Olympic competition. In the opening year of the league, she won the triple crown for batting average, home runs and runs batted in.

But other players were coming along now; the Blue Diamonds had a third base player who was a home run terror and a second base player with soft hands in the field and a sweet swing at the plate. And Mac was in her thirties now.

Mac wasn't accustomed to attention being elsewhere. The haughtiness sharpened. It seemed to jab right into the gut of the Boston Colonials and especially into me.

Mac came up to bat with the first game of the series on the line.

The score was tied at 3–3, with one out in the eighth inning. The Blue Diamonds had runners at the corners, and both of them were looking cocky.

The stadium was boogeying, the fans as loud as groupies at a rock concert. Not to steal a line or anything, but they'd put up even money now with MacDonnell at the bat.

The pitcher threw a sinker. Mac tapped a roller toward the shortstop. The runner on third broke for home.

The shortstop fielded cleanly and went for a double play to end the inning. The second base player took the toss and pirouetted to make the throw to me.

I was stretched-stretched-stretched as far as I could, barely balanced against the bag, when Mac's foot came hooking around mine and flipped me off-balance and I tumbled.

It was clearly deliberate. I rolled over and looked to the umpire for the interference call that would give us the third out and get us out of the inning with the score still tied. Instead, the umpire signaled Mac safe.

I came off the dirt in a fury.

"What do you mean, safe?" I shouted. "It was interference!"

"The runner is safe," the umpire snarled back.

Mac was standing on the bag, looking bored. The crowd was hollering things at me that I wouldn't have wanted my mother to hear, and my coach was sprinting from the dugout before I could do any more damage. But she wasn't quick enough.

"What the hell's the matter with you? This isn't the Olympics anymore!" I screamed.

Mac came alive and fired her MX-missile stare at me. The umpire shouted, "You're gone, pal!" and thumbed me out of the game.

I drop-kicked my glove toward the dugout. Some fan threw a handful of Good & Plenty candy at me, and the whole stadium resounded with the pound-pound-pound of feet stamping in time to a chant: "Ivory clean! Ivory clean!" It was the fans' endearing way of saying I was headed for the showers.

My teammates were as angry as I was. In the top of the ninth, they batted around, scoring four runs and winning the ballgame 7–4.

I did not go straight to the showers. I wish I had, because then I would not have been raging in the locker room when the sportswriters came in, trying to shade that greedy and eager look in their eyes as they circled like vultures and hoped I would give them the good quote they craved. I did.

"Mac MacDonnell is a freakin' coward," I told them. "She'll knock an infielder down and then go stand all safe and pristine out in center field, where the only thing that can attack her is maybe a mosquito. On a warm night."

The next morning, the headline in the hometown newspaper read, "Smokey O-pines: Mac's Cowardly Attack!"

Then I got traded to the Delaware Blue Diamonds.

Like a Christian who's been traded to the lions.

CHAPTER TWO

I've been called Smokey ever since I was caught with a cigarette in the seventh grade. I didn't mind the detention, but my gym teacher, who cared, pinned me against the lockers and made me feel like a sinner in the hands of an angry God. I never touched another one.

My full name is Brenda Constance O'Neill. I was named for my father, Brendan Conrad O'Neill, who was a minor league pitcher for the Albuquerque Dukes. He was expecting to be called up any day to the big leagues, when he unleashed a mighty fastball from the mound and toppled over dead from a freak brain aneurysm.

My mother was pregnant with me at the time, so I know my father only by his minor league baseball card, by the glove my mother keeps in a glass case, and by the name he left me.

I grew up in Newtown Square, Pennsylvania, a suburb of Philadelphia. Like most kids, I played Little League baseball. And when Mac MacDonnell blasted that Olympian grand slam, I was hooked for life.

I went to college down the road at West Chester University. As you can probably tell, I majored in English with a lot of history thrown in. I did pretty well, but all I really wanted to do was to play ball. My mother insisted that I finish school, and then the Boston Colonials, with a left-handed first base player and another left-handed hitter in their lineup, and seeking a little speed on the base paths, offered me a tryout. The signing bonus was the first extra money my mother and I ever had.

I was platooned at first in my rookie year, facing right-handed pitchers and building a reputation as a leadoff hitter, capable of hitting singles with two strikes on me or waiting out walks. My fielding was sharp and sure.

I had all the makings for a promising career. I should have minded not at all that I was playing for Coach Julia Pettibone, but I did.

Coach Pettibone could take a great team and make it good. She was a control freak, and I was always the type that needed a lot of room.

More than anything else, Coach Pettibone distrusted ballplayers she thought were too chummy with the press, and I basically like sportswriters. They may not be able to hit or throw as well as the players, but many of them are serious students of the game and worth talking to.

There was bound to be a problem in the mix of Coach Pettibone, sportswriters and me, and there was.

Sportswriters have a living to make and generally will not go out of their way to antagonize you. But there is one lesson that every athlete must learn: Never trust a sportswriter who is leaving the beat.

A sportswriter on her way out has nothing to lose. The little jokes you've been telling her that never went farther than her ears become fair game for her copy. She won't ever see you again, and she can make her exit with one blockbuster of a story. No doubt it has been eons since you remembered to tell her, "This is off the record."

I learned my lesson from Bobbie Bellows, when she quit her sportswriting job at the Boston *Globe* to become an editor in Arizona. I was one of three players who met with Bobbie and some other sportswriters after a game to say good-bye.

We had won, but it wasn't pretty. Coach Pettibone had left our starting pitcher in too long, and she was having one of those days when she didn't feel like pinch-hitting for anybody. We had to come back to win.

I was frustrated but trying to laugh it off. When Bobbie said something about the game's managerial decisions, I cracked, "Nobody would be better than Coach Pettibone."

Bobbie Bellows knew exactly what I meant, and so did everybody else sharing the bar tab. She wrote a devilish column about "Coach Nobody of the Boston Colonials." I was quoted. Since there were witnesses, I couldn't deny it.

I have to say, I thought the column was funny. Coach Pettibone did not.

Not too much later, I was traded.

Anyway, that is why Coach Pettibone shredded a cigarette and said, "I don't mind telling you that this is one of the happiest days of my life," when she sent me on my way, even though she was only getting a suspect relief pitcher in return. It is why she was particularly happy that I was going to the Delaware Blue Diamonds, archrivals or not, the day after I insulted the Great American Hero who was the fiercely proud star of the team.

CHAPTER THREE

I felt like I was walking the plank as I trudged down the runway to the Delaware Blue Diamonds' clubhouse. I kept thinking about what I had said to the bloodthirsty press corps: "Mac MacDonnell is a freakin' coward. She'll knock an infielder down and then go stand all safe and pristine out in center field, where the only thing that can attack her is maybe a mosquito. On a warm night."

My words were reported by newspapers, on television and radio. There was no doubt I had said them. And meant it. What was I supposed to do now, walk in and say, "Hi, guys, just kidding"?

My stomach was coiling like a sick snake. I shoved the door as if pushing aside an unwanted suitor and went in to face the Blue Diamonds.

They were waiting for me.

Their eyes had the look of a firing squad — and one that enjoyed its work. I made sure I didn't blink.

I picked out the players I recognized.

There was Tracy Moore, the third base player and one of the most intimidating women in the league. She had a monstrous batting swing that had her leading the division in home runs, but she was better known for her habit of answering sportswriters' questions with the witty quotations she had memorized as an English major. Her teammates called her Shakespeare.

She was standing with Betty Cranowski, the club's regular catcher. Cranny had a body built like a duck, and she waddled if she had to run, but from those broad-based hips she launched a fiercesome bat and a throwing arm that runners hated to challenge.

Shakespeare and Cranny, as everyone in baseball knew, had been together for years. With identical gestures, they stared at me coldly and folded their arms in front of them.

I saw Diane Sunrise, who was known as the Chief, grinning at me from a bench. A Native American, she was the Blue Diamonds' ace pitcher. Next to her, left fielder Zion Washington tied a shoe without looking up.

There might have been a touch of warmth in the

15

eyes of Beth Amos, the star second base player, called S.B. because she owned second base. She was watching a ball game on a television with shortstop Angela Gonzales and right fielder Marcia Chang. Gonzales clicked off the sound as they looked at me.

Eileen Mulligan, the first base player I would be displacing, scowled alongside Tina Corrozi, the squat backup catcher built like an old-fashioned icebox.

Mac MacDonnell was not there.

I had no trouble figuring out which locker I had been assigned. Someone had cut out the day's newspaper story and taped it there, with my quote about MacDonnell highlighted in yellow.

Everyone was watching me, saying nothing. I put my head down, walked to the locker and dropped my gear. Then I took down the newspaper clipping, tore off a strip of it, rolled it into a ball and put it in my mouth. I chewed and swallowed. I tore off another strip.

Cranowski, the catcher, was the first to laugh, a generous guffaw that set off the others.

"Eating your words, O'Neill?" said Shakespeare, and I nodded, the chuckles around me turning into eye-wiping belly laughs.

I was in.

S.B. shook my hand and said, "Welcome to the Blue Diamonds, Smokey O'Neill," and the others offered handshakes too. I was reaching for Zion Washington, the left fielder, when her expression changed and her hand dropped to her side. The group became quiet, watching me again like cynical spectators at the Roman Colosseum.

Mac MacDonnell had come in.

She had entered from the shower room and was

in front of her locker by the time I became aware of her. She was naked and utterly uncaring about it. She had small breasts and slim thighs and muscles of proud power that wreathed her arms and legs — the physique of an athlete that performed beyond pain or earthly distraction.

I noticed. She had a body that made me want to take my clothes off. Under the circumstances, it was only a passing thought.

Mac spoke before I could. "Stay clear, O'Neill. Just stay the fuck away."

Blue Diamonds' Coach DeeDee Lefevre appeared at her office door. "O'Neill," she said, "don't you think you ought to check in with the coach before you make yourself at home?"

It seemed as good a way as any to bail out. "Sure," I said.

DeeDee Lefevre was recognized universally as the best coach in the Women's Baseball League, and she had not made it the easy way. Born in a no-chance neighborhood in Philadelphia, she was rescued by one of those entrepreneur programs in which business executives offer to send schoolchildren to college if they will study, graduate and stay away from drugs. Lefevre's benefactors were two partners, one black and one white, who ran car dealerships after soldiering together in Vietnam.

Lefevre got her college education, played hockey, basketball and softball and became an athletic coach at Lincoln University in Pennsylvania. She won national recognition for building a women's sports program and was the universal choice to coach the first women's Olympic team.

There was a beautiful video, still used in all the

17

Olympic newsreels, of Mac and Lefevre taking an American flag from a spectator after the gold-medal game against the Russians and lifting it in a pose reminiscent of the Iwo Jima statue. I still got chills when I saw it.

Lefevre did not coach the next Olympic team, believing someone else should have the opportunity, but she jumped at the chance to field-manage a W.B.L. club. She and the Blue Diamonds were a perfect match. The team was based close to her home, and it was anchored by the player that Lefevre had helped to turn into a star.

Now I was in the office of this great coach, the mainspring about which this proud team wheeled. Framed pictures on the walls showed moments of Olympic and Blue Rock history, interspersed with congratulatory letters from two Presidents and numerous sports figures, politicians and entertainers.

Lefevre had three rings from coaching the Blue Diamonds to three W.B.L. Crowns. She wore one on her left hand, one on her right hand and the third on a chain around her neck.

She stood behind her desk. "Sit down, O'Neill," she said, flicking her gaze at a low couch in front of the desk. I sat. "I saw what you did out there. You're quite the charmer, aren't you?" She wasn't smiling. "Let me tell you why you're a Blue Rock. I'm the one who pushed for this trade. I need a leadoff hitter and another left-handed bat in the lineup, and you're both. Eileen Mulligan has more power than you, but you're a better fielder. She won't like sitting down, but she'll live with it, and I can use her bat coming off the bench. I gave up a pretty good relief pitcher to get you, but her

18

confidence is down and the change can't hurt her. I hope she doesn't come back to haunt me. Anyway, I've got this kid, Lynn Stryker — Stryker, don't you love it for a pitcher's name? — coming along, and I think she's good enough to beat the batters even if I give her chicken dumplings to throw. Those are the baseball reasons you're here, but there's more."

I looked at her.

"For one thing, you come cheap. Pettibone would have unloaded you for a cup of coffee and a decent excuse, so don't go thinking you're anything special on this team unless you prove it on the field. For another, this clubhouse needs something. I've got great players out there. I've got S.B., and if she isn't the most valuable player this year, she will be the next. She can hit, hit for power, run, field and throw, and she's got a sweet smile and the disposition of God's own angels. I've got a third base player who can hit me a ton of home runs, and I've got the Chief for my stopper on the mound. And I've got MacDonnell. But I need someone to jump-start this club. I've got Cranowski, who can be a clown, but it's not enough. I need someone they'll love to hate and hate to love. What you did swallowing that newspaper story — that's what I need."

Lefevre smiled briefly, and I relaxed. I shouldn't have. She wasn't finished.

"But there's one other thing, Brenda Constance Smokey O'Neill. You keep a proper distance from Mac MacDonnell, hear? If you don't, I'll take her part. Even if she's wrong, I'll take her part. She's earned that respect — from you, from me, from everyone. Someday I may do the same for you, but right now you are nothing but a Colonial castoff trying to prove your old team made a mistake. Just so we understand each other." Coach Lefevre opened her office door and called, "Miss Jewel! Come get this new player settled, would you, please?"

I hadn't said a word. Lefevre didn't even bother to ask whether I had any questions. She had simply laid it on the line her way, and that was that.

Miss Jewel, an ancient lady from Lefevre's old Philadelphia neighborhood, was at my side. She had been kind to Lefevre in her youth, and Lefevre repaid her by rescuing her from poverty to hire her as the Blue Diamonds' clubhouse manager. She was someone else for whom Coach Lefevre would always take her part.

Miss Jewel was not a fast mover, but she was dignified. She was heavy now, because in her childhood she had always been hungry. She was not educated, but she was wise, and she loved the Blue Diamonds. She loved each player the way she loved her grandchildren, and she loved the team itself in its greater meaning. She worked when she was sick, and she had never missed a game. My teammates had special extra-extra large T-shirts made for her, which she had been known to wear even to the Bright Hope Baptist Church of Philadelphia after the Blue Diamonds won their championships.

"This is a proud team, the Delaware Blue Diamonds," Miss Jewel said to me in the sweet-nectar tones of someone who has sung in a choir since she was a child.

I liked her right away. "I know. This is a homecoming for me, Miss Jewel. I grew up an hour from here, went to college forty-five minutes away. I started following women's baseball by rooting for the Blue Diamonds."

The other players were on the field for their warmup as I changed for the game. I had worn number 16 as a Boston Colonial, but in another of those wrenching little ironies, MacDonnell wore that number for the Blue Diamonds. I was assigned number 26.

As I put on my uniform, I felt like one of George Orwell's characters, when Big Brother switches sides: "Oceania is at war with Eastasia. Oceania has always been at war with Eastasia."

I brainwashed myself. "You are going to beat the Colonials. You have always wanted to beat the Colonials."

I joined the team and started taking throws from the other infielders: heat-seeking missiles from Shakespeare, rising submarines from Gonzales at shortstop and perfectionistic pinpoints from S.B. that simply nested in my glove. They tested my stretch, made me scoop out of the dirt, watched me practice a swipe tag on an imaginary runner. They said nothing, but I could tell from the relaxed droop of their shoulders that I was giving them confidence. S.B. patted me on the back when we went to the dugout.

It was the last peaceful moment I had.

When the Colonials came out for practice, their bench jockeys were on me right away, and they went for my weak spot — the quote that I had given in indignation to the sportswriters.

"Hey, Smokey," they called, "did you meet any 'freakin' cowards' over there? Did you check out that 'safe and pristine' center field yet?"

At game time, the Blue Diamonds' fans booed when I was introduced, letting me know they had not forgotten the slight I had paid Mac the day before. At least no one threw Good & Plenty.

The Blue Diamonds took the field, and I had no plays in the top of the first. The Chief was on the mound, and she got a strikeout for the first out and a popup to S.B. for the second, and then Cranowski held onto a foul tip for the third.

The hometown fans still were booing in the bottom of the inning when my name was called to lead off.

"Smokey," said Coach Lefevre, "the only person who can shut them up is you."

"Right, Coach," I said. I grinned at the Colonials' pitcher and singled with satisfaction to right field, past the first base player who had been my backup.

The booing wavered but came again — the fans were entertaining themselves now — so I stole second on the first pitch to S.B., taking out Rheta Wood, my former second base teammate, with a particularly vicious slide. Rheta was offended.

"God damn it, Smokey!" she said.

The fans stopped booing. They weren't cheering, but there was a restless rush of voices as S.B. dug in at the plate. The pitcher was rattled, and S.B. walked. We had runners on first and second and Mac at bat.

Mac did not scorch the pitcher with her trademark hooligan stare. Instead, she looked at me, planted on second base, with an expression that said, "No punk like you is going to show me up."

Of late, the sportswriters had been observing that a week had passed since Mac's last home run, and could it be that the power was draining from her bat? Mac nailed a no-doubt-about-it homer that was still rising as it cleared the left field fence, and the fans went bonkers.

I crossed home plate in front of S.B., and we stood with palms out to congratulate Mac. She shook S.B.'s hand, and then every photojournalist's camera in the place whirred as Mac went by me without so much as curling her lip. I was vastly embarrassed. S.B. quickly threw an arm across my shoulders and guided me to the dugout.

"Those runs belong to you," she said generously. "You're a great addition to the team."

The Blue Diamonds were sparking. In a fury at Mac, I went three for four. Mac went four for four, and we stomped the Colonials 8–1. We were only two games behind them in the standings.

Back in the locker room, I cracked, "I don't know about the rest of you guys, but I'm undefeated in this series." I was buried under a cascade of sopping towels, caps and sweaty T-shirts.

The next day the Wilmington *News Journal,* the statewide newspaper, ran a front-page picture of Mac ignoring me at the plate. The newspaper also ran the column from the Boston sportswriter who had preserved for posterity that flippant quote: "Like a Christian who's been traded to the lions."

CHAPTER FOUR

"Grrrr!"

"Grrrrrrr!"

"Grrrrrrrrrr!"

My teammates growled and roared like lions when I entered the clubhouse, razzing me for my latest quotable quote.

What could I do? I made the sign of the cross.

Shakespeare and Zion Washington grabbed me and stood me on a bench, and then Cranny Cranowski, wearing only her underwear, sang me, from start to finish, the song of the Cowardly Lion from the *Wizard of Oz*: "When I was king of the for-RRRRRRUST!"

Mac was not there. She lay in the trainer's room, getting a massage.

Still, the ball club was humming, and in the final game of the series against Boston, we came out and did things right. Shakespeare bombed a home run in her first at-bat. I singled in the third, moved to third base on S.B.'s single and scored on Mac's sacrifice fly. We were ahead 2–0.

Boston finally got itself going and batted around in the top of the fourth to go ahead 5–2. It stayed that way until Mac boomed a three-run homer to tie the game at 5–5.

We went into extra innings, until Mac hit another one out in the eleventh to give us a 6–5 victory. Three homers in two days — suddenly she was second in the division in home runs behind Shakespeare, and the Blue Diamonds had taken two out of three from Boston and were a game out of first place.

I joined the crush of happy players at the plate as Mac circled the bases. This time she acknowledged me — sought me out, even — to grip my hand hard and say, "O'Neill, you little shit."

S.B. pulled me away. Coach Lefevre took it in with dark eyes but said nothing.

The sportswriters descended like harpies to feed off the feud between MacDonnell and me. They clutched their notebooks and their tape recorders in their clawlike hands and asked, "Smokey, why don't you like Mac MacDonnell?"

"Who says I don't like Mac MacDonnell? I have admired her since I was a child of twelve."

It was a nasty crack, and the sportswriters snickered as they scribbled in their notebooks. Mac smouldered, her eyes as dark as twin volcanoes.

Our feud had the clubhouse pulsing with nervous energy.

The next team into town after the Boston Colonials was the last-place Nashville Stars, who arrived for a three-game series and got mugged. Mac and Shakespeare hit back-to-back home runs in the first game to inspire us to victory, and then Mac and Shakespeare and Cranny hit back-to-back-to-back home runs in the second game. Humiliated, the Stars went quietly in the final game.

"One-Two-Three-Yer-Outta-Here!" the headline in the *News Journal* jeered at the Nashville players. The fans loved it, and so did we.

The Blue Diamonds were riding a five-game winning streak as the club headed out for a road trip with the New York Aces, the Indianapolis Indies and the Charleston Rebels.

What a road trip it was.

There was the game against the New York Aces that we won when S.B. became the first player in Blue Rock history to hit for the cycle, getting her home run in a dramatic final at-bat.

There was the game against Indianapolis, in which the Indies pitcher tied a W.B.L. record by striking us out nineteen times — including me, twice. But it was the sort of day that puts a pitcher in therapy. She made only four bad pitches the entire

26

game, and all of them were to Shakespeare, who hit four titanic home runs, each a solo shot. The Blue Diamonds won the game 4–2.

We won eight out of ten. Meanwhile, over in major league baseball, the men were having one of those years when the owners talk lockout and the players talk strike. The country was so tired of hearing about labor disputes that baseball fans embraced the Women's Baseball League for their summertime entertainment.

The sportswriters swarmed.

The Blue Diamonds still had a problem. The Boston Colonials, after they tucked their tails and skedaddled out of Delaware, put together a handsome little winning streak of their own. While the Blue Diamonds went eight and two, the Colonials went nine and one, leaving the Blue Diamonds two games out of first place.

We were in the division race of our lives.

CHAPTER FIVE

The Blue Diamonds were the heirs to a tradition of Delaware baseball. While the state, sandwiched as it was between Philadelphia and Baltimore, never attracted a major league club, it hosted minor league baseball — twice.

The Blue Rocks played in Wilmington in the Inter-State League from 1940 to 1952. The team was put together by Connie Mack, the longtime Philadelphia Athletics manager, and the Carpenters, a branch of the DuPont family that started the chemical company along the banks of the Brandywine River.

The Carpenters became the owners of the Philadelphia Phillies in 1943 and held onto that team for the better part of four decades, giving Delawareans a strong and affectionate identification with baseball. The Carpenters' Phillies seemed to be a perennial disappointment. However, they brought joyful delirium to the Delaware Valley by winning the National League pennant in 1950 and the World Series in 1980.

The Blue Rocks were a way station for a number of fine major leaguers — most notably Curt Simmons and Robin Roberts, stalwarts of the 1950 Phillies' pitching staff. The club even had its own Chief in Chief Bender, a former Athletics' pitcher who was the Blue Rocks' first manager.

The team was disbanded as a consequence of its success. With the Carpenters' ownership of the Phillies, and with Simmons and Roberts pitching there, Delawareans' interests turned to the big league club. From a high of 175,000 fans in 1947, Blue Rock attendance dwindled to 26,000 in 1952.

It was time to fold. The team did, for 41 years.

By then, major league baseball had become too businesslike and too expensive, and free agency grated on the fans. They needed to believe again in something closer to home, and minor league baseball experienced a resurgence. Wilmington built a cozy little ballpark of red brick and snared a farm team from the Kansas City Royals' organization. It was named the Blue Rocks, after the earlier team, and night after night the stands were filled with fans enjoying the simple pleasure of watching young men live the dream of playing ball.

The Blue Rocks were so successful that Delaware was a natural for the Women's Baseball League. There were plenty of fans to share.

The Delaware Blue Diamonds were based in Du Pont Stadium in the sports complex at the University of Delaware in Newark. The ballpark was near the university's football field, home of the Fightin' Blue Hens, in the vicinity of "The Bob," the nickname for the Bob Carpenter Center, a basketball-and-entertainment arena named for R.R.M. Carpenter, Jr. He was the first president of the original Blue Rocks, one of the family members to own the Phillies and a longtime university trustee.

Homecoming for the women of the Delaware Blue Diamonds was triumphant, after the eight-and-two road trip. The accounts in the *News Journal* were rhapsodic, and the fans were in a swoon. There was some speculation that trading for that first base player from Boston might have given the team the jolt it needed.

The New York Aces were in town to start the homestand, and fans were filling the stadium long before game time. As the Blue Diamonds headed for the dugout after batting practice, I noticed a little fellow in the stands wearing a Blue Diamonds' jersey with the number 26 on it. It was the first time I had seen anyone wearing my number, and it gave me the shivers.

"They must have been out of Mac's number in

30

his size," said the Chief, who never said *anything*. It made me laugh.

I couldn't help but watch the little fellow during the game. He had popcorn in the first inning, a hotdog in the fourth and ice cream in the fifth. His mother faithfully kept a scorecard and showed him what she was writing. His unknown identity remains one of the sweet mysteries of my life.

The kid got his money's worth that day. The game was a tense one. I tripled my second time up and scored on S.B.'s sacrifice fly, and the Blue Diamonds led 1–0.

The score stood, going into the top of the ninth with the Aces coming to bat. Both teams had wasted numerous opportunities, and all the players had a feeling that something had to bust lose.

Stryker was pitching in relief for the Blue Diamonds. The Aces' first batter fanned, but the second batter doubled. Then the umpire called a questionable balk on Stryker, and her concentration went. She walked the next batter on four pitches.

There were Aces on first and third with one out. S.B. strolled in from second base to chat with Stryker and, we learned later, to try to calm her down.

"Just throw strikes," S.B. said. "We'll catch anything they hit."

Stryker took the advice to heart. With the runners going, the batter swung at Stryker's first offering and launched a rocket of a liner toward right field. It should have gone for a double or triple, but I was guarding the line. With a desperation stab, I caught the ball on the tip of my glove, the whiteness peeking over the soft tan webbing, and then lunged to first base before the runner could scramble back.

Double play. The Blue Diamonds won 1–0.

The fans were roaring my name. "Smokey! Smokey O!" they cried, as my teammates came running with their congratulations.

Stryker hugged me. "I owe you a dinner," she said. Then she hugged S.B. "I guess you did mean it, that you all could catch anything they'd hit!" she said.

It was bliss.

If I could have found that little fellow with number 26 on his jersey, I would have given him the game ball.

I was late in leaving the clubhouse after the game. Miss Jewel was straightening up and most of the lights were off by the time I walked out.

I didn't have much to go home to. Before we left on the road trip, I had rented a furnished room in Newark for temporary quarters. I was still arranging to have my belongings shipped from Boston.

There was a woman waiting by the players' exit. I glanced at her, intending to walk on, but she was looking at me so frankly that she caught my gaze.

"Smokey O," she said.

"Yes?"

"My name is Claire Belle. Most people call me Clarabelle — or worse. I'm a freelance writer. Usually I do pieces on rock stars or fallen politicians, but *Sports Illustrated* wants me to do something on the surging Blue Diamonds."

She had my attention for sure.

"Can we talk? How about over dinner?" she said.

"How do I know you're for real?"

She flashed me a very patronizing smile. "Suspicion is not becoming in one so young," she said, but she went fishing in a voluminous handbag. It was a designer purse, fashioned from soft leather, and she extracted from it press credentials identifying her with *Sports Illustrated.* Then she thrust a clipping, torn from *Time* magazine, at me. It was a piece on her, displaying her photo and declaring her the grande dame of rock gossip.

"We could talk over dinner," I said.

"Good. I'll drive."

I dropped a step behind to look her over. She was utterly chic, from the soft, pastel green, two-piece summer dress she wore with a green scarf around her neck to her bracelet with matching earrings. Her vanity was her tawny hair, which fell in ringlets to her shoulders. In another day and age, she would have worn white gloves.

If the *Time* magazine story hadn't said she was fifteen years older than I was, I never could have guessed.

She drove a white Mercedes, and she made it perform.

"I'm not exactly dressed for dinner," I said as I admired her driving. I was wearing white slacks and a collarless blue shirt.

"I told you, I write about rock stars. I write about rock stars who insist upon dressing like ragamuffins when they have the money to buy out the Pentagon. I am adept at finding unself-conscious bistros" — she said it with a French accent — "with elegant cuisine but no dress code. I think Buckley's Tavern will suit."

I knew Buckley's from my student days at West Chester University. It was a country tavern near the Pennsylvania line in Centreville, a small and understated gateway to Chateau Country, where the Du Ponts and other well-heeled Delawareans had their estates.

"You must know this area pretty well," I said.

"I always know where the money is."

Buckley's wasn't crowded. Clarabelle suggested a table in the bar near a window. The room was dimly lit, and the flicker of a candle on the table turned her earrings into starfire.

She ordered everything nouvelle. I ordered everything filling. I was famished from the ball game, and I wasn't buying.

When the wine was served, she took out a notebook, but she didn't ask me any questions. Instead, she explained that she had ordered this particular bottle of white Bordeaux because it reminded her of a funny experience. It happened several years ago, when she was interviewing August Summer, the lead singer of Cold War, a rock group on the way to stardom with its first number one song.

"August was a tramp. He thought he was counterculture, but he was simply dirty. And rude. He wore jeans so disreputable that the zipper was wearing out. I was interviewing him over dinner at a little inn on the Eastern Shore in Maryland, where I had to bribe the maitre d' to let us in. August kept adjusting his zipper and managed finally to get the tablecloth caught in it. When he stood up to go to the men's room, he started dragging the tablecloth and everything on the table with him — including the white Bordeaux, which spilled all over him. He was standing there in a half-crouch, with his hands clawing at his groin, which was soggy with white wine. He was tugging at the tablecloth to pull it out, hissing all the while, 'Shit! Piss! Motherfucker!' Need I say that I used that little incident as the opening for my story on Cold War? It won many awards."

I was laughing so hard that people were turning around and laughing too, from watching. The story was funny enough, but when Clarabelle, who was just as elegant as she could be, imitated this crude brute saying, "Shit! Piss! Motherfucker!" I was a goner.

Dinner was served, but Clarabelle kept dishing up the anecdotes. I could not recall a more enchanted evening. I had starred in the ball game, I was drinking a wonderful wine, and I was hearing terrific stories.

We were having coffee and dessert when Clarabelle checked her watch. "Look at the time! I haven't asked you one question! Listen, I'm staying at the new hotel and convention center near Longwood Gardens. Will you come have a nightcap with me?"

It figured that Clarabelle was staying near Longwood, the world-class gardens conceived by Pierre Du Pont, perhaps the most famous member of the family. He was president of the Du Pont Co., president of General Motors and a generous benefactor of the University of Delaware, in addition to creating the exquisite gardens, fountains and conservatory in Kennett Square, Pennsylvania.

I was getting the message that Clarabelle had more on her mind than a story about the Delaware Blue Diamonds.

I went. As we sipped after-dinner drinks, Clarabelle said, "I've got a suite upstairs. Why don't you stay, and we can talk by the pool tomorrow? I'll have you back in Newark in time."

"All right. I'll stay," I said.

The elevator we rode to her floor was glass, in full view of the lobby. I was disappointed. It meant I had to delay the way I wanted to look at her.

Her suite had two double beds in it. They had been turned down by a maid with the customary mints on the pillows. Clarabelle unwrapped one and put it in my mouth.

I reached for her hips, but she batted my hands away. "No," she said. "Let me. Go and sit down."

I took a chair next to the bed. Clarabelle unbuttoned her blouse and dropped it on the floor. She slipped off her skirt and discarded her bra and panties. She left the green scarf fastened around her neck, and it drove me wild.

Her body was young-looking and firm, a little rounded in the breasts and hips. The tail of her scarf floated against her right nipple and flowed away.

My breathing was as heavy as though I'd been sprinting. With a seductive smile, Clarabelle came to me, her hips swaying. One knee went on the chair between my thighs as she bent to kiss me, her lips molding to mine.

She put her hands on my forearms to pin them

down, and I was getting the idea that she wanted to be in charge here.

It was fine with me. I relaxed and leaned back, Clarabelle drawing closer to me. We stayed that way for some time, kissing. Her breasts were near but not touching, and her knee was almost in my crotch, but not quite. When I couldn't stand it anymore, I whimpered.

Clarabelle released me and unknotted the green scarf. I watched in raw desire. She looped the scarf behind my neck and tugged steadily, guiding me from the chair to stand before her. It was one of the sexiest moments of my life.

I couldn't be denied any longer. I clasped her hips and kissed her fiercely.

"Let me get your clothes off," she said, and I did. I wanted her so much I was trembling.

"You seem so anxious," she teased. "What is this, your first time?"

I thought about my senior year in high school and the student teacher who kept me after class because I was clowning around in gym, then seduced me in the towel room. I thought about the field hockey player I had lived with for a semester and a half at college. I thought about the tennis tournament in Boston where I met a woman who recognized me and took me to a hotel room, without ever letting me know her name.

"You're not the first," I said, "just the most tempting."

We tumbled onto the bed.

I am embarrassed to say that as soon as she touched me, I came, shuddering and gasping.

Clarabelle rolled off me. "Ball players," she said

contemptuously. "They come quick if they win, never if they lose. You get more turned on by hitting home runs than by having sex, don't you?"

"Not me," I said. "I don't hit home runs."

Clarabelle was sitting on the bed, her tantalizing legs dangling over the side. I slipped off and knelt on the floor.

"Please. Give me another chance," I said, kissing the inside of her thighs many times.

She seemed to ignore me, but her body betrayed her. Her legs twitched, and her chest heaved.

"Get back up here," she said.

I traced the sensuous outline of her breasts and waist and hips. My lips followed, caressing where I had touched her, until she laced her hands in my hair, drew my mouth to hers and held my head there.

I reached down and found her slippery and eager, and then we were rolling on the bed, sweaty and passionate, with her hot sighs urging me to get on with it, get on with it, get on with it.

Afterwards, as I lay in the dark, still inhaling the scent of her, I wondered what Clarabelle wanted from me. She wasn't the type to do anything for free.

I bought a swimsuit at the hotel shop the next morning, and we had coffee by the pool during one of those beautiful summer mornings before the humidity rises like an evil spirit.

In her swimsuit, Clarabelle didn't *look* fifteen years older than I did, and she moved so well that anyone at the pool — man or woman — gazed at her as she passed by.

Finally, she got to her questions about the Women's Baseball League and the Boston Colonials and the Delaware Blue Diamonds.

"What's Jill MacDonnell like in the locker room before a game?" she asked.

"What's this 'Jill MacDonnell' stuff? Nobody calls her that. Before a game, she prepares for it mentally. She doesn't mix much. She keeps to herself."

"How did you feel in the game against the Colonials, when she won it with a homer in the eleventh inning and then called you 'a little shit'?"

I felt stung. "How did you find out about that?"

"I have my sources. You're confirming it?"

"I guess I already did, didn't I? But she won the game for us, she can say what she wants. Mac can carry the team, if she's on."

It was really a very simple interview and didn't last long. I wanted to go back to bed with her, but she wouldn't. Clarabelle drove me back to the ballpark and was on her way.

S.B. was putting on her uniform when I walked in. "Smokey, where have you been? I tried to reach you. It was such a sensational morning that I thought you might want to come in early and go for a run with me," she said.

"I've been having a strange time of it," I said, and told her about Clarabelle.

S.B., whose countenance never seemed to darken, looked vastly troubled. "Smokey, don't you know who she is? Clarabelle and Mac used to be together."

"Oh my God."

"They met in college. Clarabelle wrote, Mac played ball. Clarabelle got a job at *USA Today* during Mac's first appearance in the Olympics, because Mac wasn't giving interviews and Clarabelle promised she could get one. Then *USA Today* kept her on to write about fidgety personalities. She made a name for herself, and now she earns a ton of money just by free-lancing. Mac and Clarabelle split up about a year ago. I don't know why, but I heard it was pretty nasty."

"This is unreal. I figured Clarabelle had some ulterior motive, but I never would have guessed in a million years she was using me to get back at Mac."

"Clarabelle is deadly. There's no doubt she'll make sure Mac hears about this."

"And then what?"

"That's the question, isn't it?"

CHAPTER SIX

After the Blue Diamonds' tense 1–0 victory over the New York Aces, we lost the next two games to them. They were the first back-to-back losses since I was traded.

In the first defeat, we simply were stymied by a hot pitcher. In the second loss, though, the Blue Diamonds had one of those herky-jerky days when the team was out of synch and misfiring. We stranded runners, botched double plays and got caught stealing. If we were a car, somebody would have taken us in for a tune-up.

We may have been looking ahead to the next series, a four-game stand against the Boston Colonials in their ballpark. But we sure weren't making it easy for ourselves.

After the first loss, Stryker offered to buy the dinner that she had promised me. We went to the Deer Park, a legendary restaurant and tavern on Main Street in Newark. Its claim to fame was that Edgar Allan Poe was said to have stayed there, and its interior was still as dark as a midnight dreary where you could ponder, weak and weary. It was a good place to go after you'd been roundly overmatched by a pitcher.

The Deer Park was favored by Blue Diamonds' players, and the management served us our drinks at half price — if we had to buy them ourselves. Usually the clientele picked up the tab for us, paying the going rate. As far as the management was concerned, we were a profitable attraction.

I was learning about the difference between playing in Boston and playing in Delaware.

Boston was big and impersonal. The Colonials had to compete with the other professional sports teams — men's baseball, football, hockey and basketball — for attention.

Boston was splintered into its own societies, like the academics, the bankers, the politicians and the theatre and arts crowd, and they rarely mixed.

In Delaware, a state so small that you could drive the length of it in two hours, everyone cared passionately about everything. Politicians supported the university's basketball team; chemical company executives helped to organize the annual flower show for charity. Million-dollar lawyers played in the softball leagues, and everybody went to the Delaware State Fair.

In this atmosphere, the Blue Diamonds mattered and the players were celebrities. When Stryker and I walked into the Deer Park, we were recognized and exclaimed over.

A Chrysler worker was quicker with a ten-dollar bill than a university professor was, and won the privilege of buying us a round of beer.

"To the heroes of yesterday's game," the Chrysler worker toasted.

"It would have to be yesterday's. There were no heroes today," I said, a little sardonically.

"Nothing you can do when you run into a pitcher like that," the professor said.

We drank and talked baseball, and the professor and I chatted about her colleagues at West Chester University whose classes I had taken. After a while, Stryker and I drifted off to find a table.

I was still smarting from the day's loss. I had gone hitless.

"It must be nice to be a relief pitcher," I said. "You don't have any responsibility at all for a game like today's."

"Oh, yeah, Smokey, being a relief pitcher is just a bed of roses. Do you have any idea what it's like walking back into the clubhouse if you've blown a lead and lost the game?"

"Pitchers. You think nothing happens without you."

"Oh, yeah? Then why am I buying you this dinner?"

"Guilt," I said.

"Maybe." Stryker looked thoughtful. "Smokey, Clarabelle interviewed me, too."

"Word is getting around, I see."

"I didn't get the kind of five-star treatment you got." Stryker gave me a very speculative look.

I knew I was blushing and hoped it didn't show in the Deer Park's dark and gloomy light.

"You didn't know about her and Mac?" Stryker asked.

"Honest to God, Stryker, I didn't. Not then."

"I didn't know, either, when she asked me for an interview. She told me she was with *Sports Illustrated,* so I talked to her."

"What did she ask you about?" I said.

"It didn't seem like much at all. She asked a lot of questions about Mac and a lot of questions about you. It was nothing real penetrating, but I hear she can twist things."

"She's a manipulator, that's for sure."

"Would you have gone to bed with her if you knew she'd been with Mac?"

"She was pretty sexy, Stryker."

"Even if you knew it would make Mac mad?"

"How could I tell?"

Stryker laughed uncomfortably. "Smokey, why can't you lay off her?"

"Why can't she lay off me?"

"Smokey, we're talking about Mac MacDonnell. You and I are on the same team as *Mac MacDonnell.*"

"I know. I read the box scores."

"Come on, Smokey, lighten up."

I did, and we had a pleasant evening together.

But I was getting damned tired of Mac's shadow falling across everything I did.

After the second straight loss to the New York Aces, I was helmet-throwing, trash-can-kicking frustrated. I had missed a low throw from Gonzales at shortstop, and although the official scorer gave her the error, it was a play I had expected to make myself.

Also, I had gone hitless again, contributing nothing more than a ground ball to move a runner to the next base. It was not the performance I wanted as a prelude to my first trip to Boston in a visiting team's uniform.

After the game, I sulked in the dugout, not wanting to talk to sportswriters or teammates in the locker room. The murky dusk darkened into night, and the glaring stadium lights cast the ballpark in stark, strange shadows.

Finally, I went in. I thought everyone had gone, even Miss Jewel. I slammed my glove down on the bench and bent to untie a shoe.

Then Mac appeared. She was still in her uniform, as I was, the number 16 on her jersey reminding me who carried the clout around here. She had a basket of baseballs with her.

"Can you throw BP?" she said.

"Yes," I said. I had pitched batting practice on occasion for my college team.

"Then come on."

I was as confused as I had ever been. Mac clearly had waited around for me. If she wanted to hit, any player could have thrown balls for her. Whatever this was, it had to do with me.

Mac had not exactly been in the best frame of mind. As bad a series as I had, Mac's was worse. I had tripled, scored the only run and made the game-saving play in the first game, before my play went south. Mac had made a rare mental error in the field, letting a ball get over her head for a triple in the last game, and she had failed to drive in any runs, which was what she got paid to do.

I was a second-year player, and I expected to be better tomorrow than I was today, and better still the day after. A slump for me was simply a slump. A slump for Mac caught the sportswriters' notice, and you wondered whether her breathtaking talent was bleeding from her, siphoned away by the real prince of thieves, time.

We stepped onto the field and into the blind and pitiless stare of the stadium lights. I went to the mound, she to the plate. She settled into the batting stance that I had imitated as a young fan and nodded at me to start throwing.

Crraaccckkk! My first pitch she ripped right back at me, and if I hadn't gotten my glove up by luck and by reflex, I would have made a team of dentists very busy and very rich for a long time.

The second pitch zoomed past my right ear, and the third blasted at my feet and had me skipping out of its way.

I held the fourth ball in my hand and glared at her, but she was setting herself nonchalantly for the next pitch. I wasn't *that* stupid — I knew she was doing this on purpose. I decided I'd rather not appear to be intimidated and kept on pitching. The fourth ball I caught just before it hit me in the gut.

Mac was an impresario with that bat, making the ball do what she wanted, forcing me to dodge and duck and deflect.

I thought about throwing at her but didn't. It seemed somehow the wrong thing to do, and so I let her go on straightening me up and knocking me down as she sprayed my pitches back through the middle.

There was one ball left. My nerves were gone. I threw it and bailed off the mound, only to see it soar high above my head into the center field seats. I felt very foolish.

I was sweaty and exhausted and sore. Mac looked tired and serene, but then she spoke and I knew what she was keeping inside.

"I heard about you and Claire Belle," she said.

"Mac, I didn't know."

"She knew," Mac said.

Without another word, without another look, Mac headed toward the clubhouse.

I'd had it.

"Mac," I hollered, my voice harsh and dying in the stadium shadows, "it's not my fault if you couldn't keep her."

She never stopped. There was no hitch in her shoulders, no hesitation in her step, as she walked away.

And I knew this mess with Mac, Clarabelle and me wasn't over yet.

47

CHAPTER SEVEN

I had trouble sleeping that night. I dreamed about those batted balls zooming at me at supersonic speed, while I dodged in sick slow motion. I awoke in such a sweat that I had to change the T-shirt I was sleeping in.

We were due at the ballpark early the next day for a charter flight from the Greater Wilmington Airport to Boston for a showdown with the Colonials.

The pressure was on. We had lost those two games in a row to the New York Aces, and we needed to sweep the four-game series to tie Boston for first place in the division. A 2–2 split would be like kissing your sister. If we lost four straight games, the newspapers would be assigning obituary writers instead of sportswriters to cover us.

We were a little quiet at the airport. I was relieved when S.B. greeted me with a pat on the back and asked whether I had packed a bullet-proof vest for my return to Boston. She could always make me laugh when I needed to.

S.B. and I sat together on the flight, and I told her about pitching batting practice to Mac.

"I took sports psychology in college," S.B. said, "but nothing like that was in the textbooks."

"It's not fair, S.B. I mean, I didn't know about Clarabelle."

"I know, Smokey. Judging from what Mac said to you, I'd say she's not really blaming you, but she had to get it out of her system anyway." S.B. laughed. "Whatever it was, I hope you helped her regain her stroke for this series. We need her to hit."

Our flight landed, and we gathered to collect our bags. I was not paying much attention to the players milling about me, until I grabbed for my luggage and bumped against Mac reaching for hers. We drew back, the air so charged between us that I wondered why I couldn't smell the ozone.

"What is it, O'Neill?" Mac said. "You want to carry my bags?"

"Why not? This team's been carrying you all season," I said, and not very pleasantly.

I don't know where S.B. and Zion Washington came from, but they wrapped me up between them and propelled me a step or two backwards. Cranny swiveled her formidable hips in front of Mac and set herself like a sumo wrestler.

Mac was surprisingly unperturbed. "I'll tell you what, O'Neill," she said. "Let's make this interesting. Say I hit four home runs in the game today. Will you carry my bags then?"

"Four home runs?" I asked.

"Ten bucks says Mac does it," Stryker said. "Any takers?"

"Nobody hits four home runs in a game," Shakespeare said.

"You did," said Stryker. "Against Indianapolis."

"I know. I figure we only get to do that once a season, and I already did it. Ten bucks, Stryker," said Shakespeare, and they shook on it.

"Twenty bucks," I said, "that I'm on base each time Mac hits one."

"I'll take that bet," Mac said.

"Well, I'm betting against both of you. This is silly," Cranny said.

The wagers and the ante mounted. By general agreement, S.B. was put in charge of settling any disputed claims afterwards.

Just that quickly, our pregame jitters were gone.

We were giddy in the dugout. Cranny surreptitiously stuck her elbow into my side during the "Star Spangled Banner," and I dishonored the anthem and disgraced myself by falling backward onto the bench. Coach Lefevre gave me a look that said, "One more stunt and you'll be fined," but everybody else was giggling.

When my name was announced as the leadoff

batter, the Boston fans surprised me with warm applause — a gesture of thanks to a player who had departed through no disloyalty of her own.

I was touched, but my job was to turn the applause into boos and to get on base so I could win my twenty dollars from Mac.

The Colonials' pitcher looked nervous — first place was Boston's to lose — so I guessed she'd start me out with a fast ball. She did, and I walloped it back through the middle for a clean single.

Boooo, went the Boston fans. I stood on first base and stared meaningfully at Mac as she knelt in the on-deck circle. She shrugged, as if to say my hit was a fluke.

Coach Lefevre put on the hit-and-run. S.B. swung, I sprinted, and when the dust settled, I was on third and S.B. was on first and nobody was out. And Mac MacDonnell was at the plate.

The Blue Diamonds were standing in the dugout. They had a lot of money riding on this at-bat. Mac took the first pitch for a called strike. She bashed the next one over the fence in right for an opposite-field home run.

The Boston fans were deathly silent as we trotted for home, in this most improbable unfolding of events.

"Who wrote this script?" said S.B., laughing as she crossed the plate behind me.

"You'll owe me twenty bucks," I taunted Mac as she came in.

"You'll be carrying my bags," she retorted.

Our delighted teammates hugged us and pounded

us on the back. We scarcely noticed that we were up 3–0 with nobody out, in the first game of the season's most crucial series.

Shakespeare tripled, and Cranny knocked her in with a sacrifice fly. Boston yanked its humiliated starting pitcher, and the reliever did her job and got out of the inning without any more damage.

The Blue Diamonds led 4–0 and felt very complacent. The Chief was on the mound.

The Colonials went with a whimper in their half of the first inning, not even hitting a ball out of the infield. Since we had batted around, I was first up in the second.

I dropped a surprise bunt in front of the third base player and beat the throw to first. S.B. moved me to second with a groundout, and then damned if Mac didn't come up and tattoo another one into the seats. We were ahead 6–0, and the bet was still on.

In my next at-bat, I was getting nervous and was fortunate to wait out a walk. S.B. flied out, and there really was no doubt in my mind that Mac would do what she did. She homered.

We exchanged pleasantries at the plate.

"Fuck you, O'Neill," Mac said.

"Fuck you, Mac," I replied.

We were up 8–0 and having a swell time.

The Chief had a little lapse in concentration with such a lopsided score. She gave up back-to-back home runs to the heart of Boston's power-packed batting order. Even so, the Colonials' fans cheered only halfheartedly. With the score at 8–2, there wasn't much for them to enjoy except for the chill of the local brew at this long and warm night at the ballpark.

I came up again in the eighth inning with two out, and I figured I had better be aggressive if I wanted to keep my streak going. I slammed a curve ball into right field but got myself thrown out trying to stretch a single into a double.

As sure as death and taxes, Mac hit her fourth homer in the ninth. S.B., who had led off with a double, scored in front of her. The final score was Blue Diamonds 10, Colonials 2.

The locker room was a raucous place after the game. Mac had her four homers, I had gone three for three with a walk, and all that was left to do was to sort out the wagers.

"You owe me twenty bucks," Mac said.

"The hell I do!" I said. "How am I supposed to be on base when you're the second batter in the inning?"

"You've only got yourself to blame for that. You got thrown out," Mac said.

"Pay up, Smokey," Cranny said. She was mugging hilariously, her face a caricature of utter despair. "I have to pay up, so you have to pay up. Cheerfully, like me."

I took a twenty-dollar bill from my wallet and offered it to Mac. I saw the fierce pride in the glint of her dark eyes, and maybe I realized for the first time, *This is Mac MacDonnell. This is Mac MacDonnell, who was an Olympic hero, who can carry a ball club, who can hit four home runs at will.*

"My bags. Don't forget my bags," Mac said.

And I remembered: This was Mac MacDonnell, who tormented me even in my sleep.

We were playing in the dog days of summer, when the only thing that America cares about is a pennant race. Most of the newspapers in the country ran front-page photos of Mac hitting her fourth home run with that famous stroke that could bring tears of joy to a batting coach's eyes.

Our teammates chattered to the sportswriters about how Mac had predicted that she would hit four homers, and sports editors everywhere salivated for the story.

The morning news shows wanted to interview Mac, but as usual, she wouldn't agree. Coach Lefevre went on, instead, speaking confidently about the Blue Diamonds' chances of catching Boston and winning the division.

Someone asked, "What do you like best about your team?"

"I like its character," Coach Lefevre said. "It's got a little junkyard dog in it."

By game time, we were wearing T-shirts emblazoned with "Junkyard Dogs." Cranny stood on a locker room bench with Zion Washington, and they led us in a chorus of "How Much Is That Doggie in the Window?"

Mac didn't sing, but she watched. Later I saw her standing with Coach Lefevre. The coach had her arm around Mac's shoulders and appeared to be talking to her quite earnestly. Mac was looking at the floor, but she was nodding and smiling. For the first time since I had joined the club, Mac looked happy.

When we took the field for batting practice, my old pals from the Boston sportswriters' corps waylaid me, knowing I was good for a no-brainer story.

"How's Delaware?" one asked.

"Good. I like it. The sportswriters are kinder."

They laughed. "Don't you miss Coach Pettibone?" another said.

"Back off," I said. "I'm not going to say anything that could get Boston riled up. I like Delaware's chances."

"Say, Smokey," said a third, "have you noticed that Rheta Wood, your old second base pal, has been making throwing errors to first since you got traded?"

"I'm not talking about Boston," I said.

They sighed to let me know that I was hurting their feelings, hindering them from doing their jobs and taking food from the mouths of their babies.

They tried a new approach.

"So how are you getting along with your Delaware teammates?" one asked.

"Coach Lefevre said it this morning. I'm just another of the junkyard dogs. We scrap, but we win."

"What's the difference," said another, "in playing on the same team with Mac MacDonnell instead of playing against her?"

"I hadn't noticed a difference," I said.

They laughed and scribbled in their notepads. "Same old Smokey," they chuckled.

"Don't you get me into trouble," I protested. "All

I meant was that Mac MacDonnell is an intense competitor, no matter where you watch her from."

"We know what you meant," they said.

They did, too.

The ball game, the second in the series, was an old-fashioned shoot-out, in which the pitchers and the fielders were not safe and the hitters were guilty of reckless endangering.

The fans loved it. The coaches chugged Maalox.

The Junkyard Dogs, alias the Delaware Blue Diamonds, spent much of their time on the bench barking at one another. We barked our way back from a 5–1 deficit, took a 9–5 lead, fell behind 10–9, and then came back again.

When Boston came up in the bottom of the ninth, the Blue Diamonds were leading 11–10 with Stryker pitching. Boston worked her over until the Colonials had the bases loaded with one out.

Coach Lefevre crossed her arms and looked stoical. It was going to be Stryker's game to win or lose.

Coach Pettibone signaled for a suicide squeeze. The batter popped up her bunt, pushing it toward the mound. Stryker coolly let the ball drop, caught it on the bounce and threw it to Cranny at home plate.

Cranny stepped on the plate for the force-out, then threw to me at first, beating the runner by a long stride.

Double play. The Blue Diamonds won.

Stryker wrapped herself around Cranny, who

practically had to carry our emotionally drained pitcher to the locker room. The sportswriters hardly could do their interviews over the howls of the Junkyard Dogs.

I was one very contented ball player as I left the stadium. Then I happened to glance at the sportswriters' parking lot. Slipping away, like a shamefaced peeping tom, was a white Mercedes. So we were still being shadowed by Clarabelle, she of *Sports Illustrated* and the poisonous prose.

CHAPTER EIGHT

I got up early the next morning to go running. The humidity, even at that hour, was as soggy as a swamp, and so I went long and slow until my lungs were leaden and I had soaked all the tension out of my body.

When I returned steamy and sodden to the hotel, the lobby was still as quiet as daybreak, with only the most workaholic of the business travelers stirring. I poured myself a complimentary cup of coffee from the hotel's urn.

I turned as the lobby doors swished open. Mac

came in, and I swear I saw a white Mercedes pulling away.

Mac was scowling and carrying a newspaper. When she spied me, she came right over. She slapped a sports section from the Boston *Globe* onto the coffee table and pointed to a headline reading, "Junkyard Dogs Still Scrapping."

"You can't leave it alone, can you?" she said. "You let those sportswriters use you like a cheap whore. You give them whatever they want."

That was a bit much to hear. I jerked my head toward the doors, where I had seen the white Mercedes driving off, and I said, "Maybe I wasn't the only one giving it away."

Mac gave me a look that could boil water. "Someone ought to beat you until you're too tired to cry," she said.

She left me sweating with my cooling cup of coffee. I took a look at the story.

It was very sympathetic to me, the late Boston player. The sportswriter took Coach Lefevre's quote about the "junkyard dogs" and called me the "pit bull" of the pack. He said I even snarled at Mac MacDonnell, and proved his point by citing my crack from the day before, when I had said "I hadn't noticed a difference" in playing with Mac or against her.

Then the sportswriter suggested that Mac deserved to have a young pup at her heels. He speculated that Mac's best days were behind her. "Mac's bark may be worse than her bite," he wrote.

He pointed out that the Boston Colonials hadn't won a game against the Blue Diamonds since I was traded, and he questioned Coach Pettibone's judgment of talent, I'm happy to say. He made me look like a hero — and at Mac's expense.

When I got back to the hotel room that I was sharing with S.B., she was just out of the shower, a towel draped around her. She was on the telephone, saying, "Wait a minute, Coach, she's back. . . . All right, I'll tell her. 'Bye." There was concern in S.B.'s eyes as she turned to me. "Coach Lefevre wants to see you in her room. Right now."

I gestured at my drenched running clothes. "I need a shower."

"If I were you, I'd assume that 'right now' means right now," S.B. said.

"Uh-oh. You don't suppose I'm being sent back to the Colonials, do you?"

"I don't think so. She wants you to bring your checkbook."

"Guess I'm being fined for something."

"Guess so. Smokey, what have you done?"

"I don't know," I said, but I did. I remembered Coach Lefevre's words. *But there's one other thing, Brenda Constance Smokey O'Neill. You keep a proper distance from Mac MacDonnell, hear? If you don't, I'll take her part. Even if she's wrong, I'll take her part. She's earned that respect — from you, from me, from everyone.*

I guessed my latest quote to the sportswriters had really done it.

I went to Lefevre's room. Her door was open, and there was a copy of the Boston *Globe* on the bureau. The coach was waiting for me, like the sheriff at high noon.

"There is a difference," she said, "in behaving like

a junkyard dog and a dog in the manger. I won't have anyone on my team undermining other players, maligning them to the press, especially when the player is of the caliber and the quality of Mac MacDonnell. Sit down at that desk, O'Neill, and write me out a check for five hundred dollars."

"Coach, please. Five hundred dollars?"

"Don't interrupt me, O'Neill. I'm not finished. I said five hundred, and I meant five hundred. I'm not going to cash it — yet. This is earnest money. If you make any more snide remarks to the press about Mac MacDonnell, I will cash it, and you will be back writing me a new check for a thousand dollars. And if you say something again, I'll cash that thousand dollar check, and you can come back and write me one for fifteen hundred, and so on. But if you can manage to restrain yourself — hard as we all know that will be — I'll return this five-hundred-dollar check to you at the end of the season, uncashed. You have the right to say what you want, O'Neill. Just so long as you're willing to put your money where your mouth is."

I wrote her the check.

She took it and said, "You are that rare player, O'Neill, who makes me wish I had a college team again. I'd have you run laps until you dropped. Judging from the look of you" — she surveyed me in my running clothes — "that would take a good long time. You would deserve every minute of it, and probably it still wouldn't be long enough for the lesson you need to learn."

She sent me away. I wished I had dared her wrath and taken the time to shower before I saw her, because in my embarrassed and downcast state, I had to return to my hotel room where I was sure there would be yet another judgment awaiting me.

S.B. was indeed prepared for my return. She had ordered breakfast for us from room service, and the coffee smelled very good. I postponed my shower again, changing into a dry sweatshirt so I wouldn't get chilled, and sat down to eat and to hear her out.

"Well, I wasn't traded," I said.

"I didn't think you would be. Room service thoughtfully provided me with a copy of this morning's Boston *Globe*. I see that you have been granting interviews as usual. Is that what Lefevre wanted you for?"

"If Lefevre decides to leave baseball, she could make a fine living as a loan shark," I said. I told S.B. what had happened.

"Smokey, let's talk about all this. You are making your life a lot harder than it has to be."

"That's the way I do things."

"Don't give me that tough-guy routine. I'm your friend. I'm your friend because you act like you never thought you'd have one when you needed one."

It was true. S.B. smiled at me affectionately and teasingly, and I smiled back.

"Baseball is a cruel game, Smokey. Did you ever hear of a pitcher named Bo Belinsky? He threw a no-hitter once, but his lifetime record was bad, just twenty-eight fifty-one. I carry around something that he said when he retired."

S.B. retrieved a slip of paper from her wallet and read, " 'I don't feel sorry for myself. I knew sooner or later I'd have to pay the piper. You can't beat the piper, babe; I never thought I could. But I'll tell you who I do feel sorry for — all those guys who never heard the music.' "

She put the paper away. "We give our youth and vitality to the game, and in the end it's a tease and a cheat and it takes away our skills and leaves us looking like fools. It's not an easy thing to face. Mac MacDonnell is a great player, maybe the greatest ever to play women's baseball. She's facing it, Smokey. It's subtle. On any given day, she is as great as she ever was. But not on every given day. She's reminded of it every time you needle her. Can you think about that for a moment?"

"S.B., she never lets up on me. You know that. She never lets up."

"I know it. Ten years ago, five years ago, she would have dazzled you with her skills, and you would have subsided in wonder. But she can't do that now. She *can't*. Smokey, trust me. If you back off just a little, I think she will, too."

"I don't want to. It's not my way. But I'll think about it, S.B., because you asked me to and because Coach Lefevre is holding a five-hundred-dollar check that says I'd better."

S.B. laughed. "Do it for love, or do it for money. Just do it," she said.

The clubhouse was not a warm and friendly place when I walked in. No one said anything, but no one greeted me or made a joke, and the story in the Boston *Globe* wasn't taped to my locker. The Chief, who was using the locker next to mine, had her back to me as she dressed for the game.

I was getting the message that I had crossed the line. Maybe it was because we were playing in Boston against our archrivals, and what I said appeared to give aid and comfort to the enemy. Maybe my loyalty still was suspect.

Well, live and learn. If I was wrong, I was going to own up to it.

Mac, as usual, was by herself, going through whatever mental preparation she did before a game. No one ever, ever intruded.

"Mac," I blurted, and every Delaware Blue Diamond held her breath and stayed statue-still. "I shouldn't have said what I said about you. I'm sorry."

"You are," Mac said. "You are the sorriest player ever to step between the white lines."

I feared there would be no mercy for me, but S.B. tousled my hair, and Stryker patted me on the butt, and Zion Washington kissed me on the cheek.

And when I scored in the eighth inning, driven in by what would be the game-winning RBI from S.B., Mac, uncharacteristically, was waiting at the plate.

She shook my hand and looked me in the eye and said, "Nice going."

And the Blue Diamonds stood in the dugout to welcome me in.

CHAPTER NINE

Nothing inspires a headline writer like misfortune. "Diamonds Get the Carat, Boston the Stick," read the headline in the Boston *Herald* after the Colonials' third loss in a row. Their hold on first place was down to one game.

The Boston players were so tense that they were fidgeting during the national anthem. Even so, they were in the best position they could be, because first place was theirs to lose and their ace was pitching. Her name was Lorraine Jackson, but she was known as Lorraine of Terror, partly because she threw so hard and partly because she was so high-strung.

I led off the game with one of those performances that leaves you wondering whether to laugh or cry. Lorraine of Terror had me struck out swinging on a slider, but her pitch broke with such sassiness that it capered past the catcher. I ran for my life and was safe at first base, leaving my teammates shaking their heads and laughing.

Lorraine of Terror tossed her head like a spooked colt. I figured I ought to help her nerves along.

With S.B. at the plate, I sprinted toward second on a steal. Rheta Wood, my old double-play partner, remembered my last aggressive slide and was a little tentative going for the ball. It ricocheted off her glove into center field, and I wound up on third base.

My teammates were still laughing. Frustrated and furious, Lorraine of Terror obligingly balked me home. The Blue Diamonds were ahead 1–0, without so much as hitting a foul ball.

A troop of Girl Scouts in the stands pulled their berets over their eyes. Beer sales were brisk. Somebody who had brought a trumpet to play the "Charge" fanfare began to sound out "Taps" but was booed to silence.

S.B. homered, and the rout was on. The Colonials looked like cockroaches in a close encounter with a can of Raid. After nine merciless innings, it was Delaware 14, Boston 0. The teams were tied for first place.

The locker room was bedlam. The junkyard dog chorus was yapping and baying, Zion Washington and Marcia Chang were dancing to the rock music blaring from Shakespeare's portable stereo, and Gonzales was spraying shaving cream onto Cranny, who was bare to the waist and giggling helplessly.

Somehow we got ourselves dressed and onto the team bus for a ride to the Boston airport, with Shakespeare's stereo still going full blast. Players either sang along with the music or simply listened, because it was much too loud for anyone to talk. Anyway, everyone was too tired to.

Coach Lefevre had a no-alcohol rule for bus rides and flights, but it was dark and Eileen Mulligan had a flask of Irish whiskey that was passed in jolly conspiracy from teammate to teammate. The singing got louder and the smiles broader, until the flask was handed to me for the second time and I found Coach Lefevre standing over me.

Lefevre *never* walked through the bus, which is why she was able to surprise us. I was turned toward the back when I took the whiskey, and everybody was watching the flask, not the coach. Lefevre had me so cold that a jury of my relatives would have convicted me without mercy.

Lefevre glared at Shakespeare, who turned down the volume on her stereo. Then she glared at me. "I'd like to see you up front," she said.

Stryker pantomimed getting hanged as I walked by, still carrying the whiskey flask. I sat next to Coach Lefevre.

This was no time for bravado. I looked at the floor.

"I want you to know," Lefevre said, "that your play was outstanding during the Boston series. Now go back where you were and tell Mulligan to put the booze away until we land in Indianapolis and get to the hotel."

I was astonished. "That's it?"

"What were you expecting?"

"Just what you said, Coach. Honest to God." I was gone — and thankful.

My teammates — fair-weather friends, all of them — were eager to know what had befallen me.

"That was quick. What happened?" Gonzales said.

"She said Mulligan should put the booze away until we get to the hotel in Indianapolis," I said, handing the incriminating flask back to the power-hitting pinch hitter.

"That's all?" Gonzales said.

"Well, Goddamn it, Gonzo, go check for yourself if you're so interested."

"No way," said the shortstop, slinking down in her seat. "I wouldn't go near Coach Lefevre in the dark unless I had garlic and a silver stake."

That got us laughing. Cranny did a Count Dracula imitation, flapping her arms, moaning, "Blood, blood," in a campy accent and falling on Shakespeare's neck. Shakespeare shoved her away, but Cranny may have left teeth marks.

My head was buzzing gently from Mulligan's Irish whiskey. I wanted another swallow, but not enough to be foolhardy about it. Instead, I cracked open a soda that I had brought from the ballpark and hunkered down in my seat next to S.B. Shakespeare turned up the volume on her stereo, although not enough to agitate Coach Lefevre.

The song was "Crystal in Time," by the NaySayers. It had lyrics that could make your heart stop and a melody that made you wish it would. The chorus went:

> "This night should never have to end.
> Let's savor one last glass of wine,
> And if we never meet again,
> At least we had this crystal in time."

I was surrounded by sleepy and slightly drunken teammates. We were on a dark stretch of highway, with the road noises locked out of the bus and the brightest constellations burning through Boston's nightlight.

"S.B.," I said.

"What?"

"It doesn't get much better than this, does it?"

"Nope. What did Lefevre say to you?"

"She said to put the booze away."

"What else?"

"I'm embarrassed to say. Anyway, you won't believe me."

"Try me."

"She said my play was outstanding during the Boston series."

"It was."

"It's because of you, S.B. I feel great at the plate because I know you're hitting behind me. You move me along if I get on or pick me up if I don't. And I feel great in the field because I know you're there to make the plays and keep us anchored in the infield."

"Thank you, Smokey. But the Blue Diamonds weren't a first-place team until you got here."

"I mean it, S.B. You should be the M.V.P."

She laughed and put her arm around my

shoulders, and I lay back and sipped my soda until the bus dropped us at the airport and we boarded a charter flight for Indianapolis.

Lefevre or no Lefevre, Mulligan offered around her flask after we were airborne. It was passed more secretively this time, across the rows of contented ball players. I was sitting between S.B. and Zion Washington. Above the whispery rush of the engines, Zion hummed songs from the old civil rights movement, singing about how "We Shall Overcome" and "Keep Our Eyes on the Prize." I felt a sweet sense of yearning.

And then I felt a shock of nerves. I had forgotten. I had a bet to pay off.

Our luggage had been collected at the hotel and taken directly to the airport, but we were responsible for our own gear once we landed in Indianapolis. I was jittery for the rest of the flight.

At the baggage claim area, I took a breath — one of those deep ones that coaches teach you to calm yourself down — and approached Mac. I could never tell what she was going to do.

"Where are your bags?" I said.

She looked me over, as though she was considering a poker hand she couldn't decide whether to keep or throw in.

"I thought you might welch," she said.

"Not me. I pitch batting practice, I carry bags, whatever it takes to win ball games."

"You are so full of it," Mac said, but she had drunk from Mulligan's magic flask and there was no malice in her words.

I started to juggle Mac's luggage and mine, wondering how I would manage it all, when Stryker appeared and took a bag, and so did Gonzales and Shakespeare and Marcia Chang.

"Four home runs," Gonzales said. "I think we can all appreciate that."

S.B. had a dream series against Indianapolis. In three games she went nine for twelve, with three home runs, a triple, two doubles and three singles. I was so impressed that I wouldn't even let her get up to change the television channels in our hotel room. I did it for her.

S.B. ended the series two points behind Rheta Wood for the best batting average in the division, and she got top billing on "Baseball Week in Review" on the Sports News Network.

Her performance made it easy for the rest of us. We swept the Indies. Meanwhile, Boston dropped two out of three to the New York Aces, falling two games out of first place.

We were feeling quite giddy — which is why we were puzzled when Coach Lefevre summoned us for a team meeting in the hotel lobby before our morning flight to Charleston. Team meetings rarely meant good news.

Lefevre looked solemn as we gathered, and when she spoke, her voice carried in it the bell-like tones of muted sorrow. "Miss Jewel will not be making the trip to Charleston with us," she said. "She had chest pains and was taken to the hospital. She's been flown back home to Philadelphia for treatment."

The veterans on the team — Mac, the Chief, Shakespeare and Cranny — looked particularly stricken. The Blue Diamonds had never played a game without Miss Jewel.

"She's expected to recover fully," Coach Lefevre said. "She wants all of you to play your best. Her daughter Melinda will meet us in Charleston to fill in for her."

We felt helpless. Baseball teams are celebrations of youth and health, where the worst casualties are broken bones and bruised egos. Matters of life and death are not admitted there.

Cranny organized us to go into the hotel gift shop and buy get-well cards. Marcia Chang collected our contributions for the most expensive flower arrangement the florist could create. It wasn't enough, but it was all we could do at the time.

We flew into Charleston and got settled at our hotel. We had some time to kill before our night game with the Rebels, so S.B., Stryker, Zion Washington and I decided to go sightseeing.

Charleston is one of those cities that is exotic in a Southern sort of way. Its houses, centuries old, have their front doors turned away from the narrow streets as if they have a secret they don't wish to share, and they conceal it further with sprays and sprays of honey-sweet flowers that divert your attention.

"What do you suppose happened in some of these places?" I said as we wandered down cobblestoned alleyways. "In which one did the embarrassed family hide the crazy nephew in the attic? Where did the master of the house kiss the serving girl when no one was looking? And what did the daughter do after she got the note from her lover saying, 'Flee. All is discovered'?"

"What do you do in your spare time, Smokey? Write bad gothic novels?" Stryker needled.

"The problem with pitchers is they have no imagination. If there wasn't a catcher behind the plate, they wouldn't even know what pitch to throw," Zion said. "Smokey, you go right ahead and talk. I'm listening."

"Smokey's got an imagination, all right," S.B. said, her eyes alive with mischief. "You ought to hear her talking in her sleep."

"I don't talk in my sleep!" I protested.

"Then why are you blushing?" Stryker said. "What does she say, S.B.?"

"I think I've violated the trust between roomies enough," S.B. said. "But I'll tell you this. Some nights it would be a waste of money to put the pay-for-porn movies on the hotel TV."

"You're making this up!" I said, but they barely heard my words through their laughter. I gave up and laughed with them.

We had an extraordinary day. We took a boat ride to Fort Sumter, where Abner Doubleday, the legendary father of us all, was a soldier when the first shots of the Civil War were fired. We had a carriage ride behind an old horse named Buck — a slow-footed beast retired from Disney World, according to the woman who drove him. She was a Charleston native, and when she pronounced the horse's name, it had about three syllables in it: "Ba-ooo-uck."

When we weren't joking around, we worried desperately about Miss Jewel.

CHAPTER TEN

The fickleness of the South Carolina coastal weather caught up with us, and a rain as soft and persistent as Southern charm washed out our game.

Rain dripped from drooping trees and puddled on cement sidewalks and close-clipped lawns. Bright petals fell into the gutters, and the façades of antebellum buildings darkened as the rain soaked in. Passersby became faceless under the stretched skins of their umbrellas, and taxi drivers picked up extra fares.

Blue Diamond players gathered in the hotel lobby

and stared disbelievingly at the weather. What were we to do, if not play baseball?

"Y'all look like little lost puppies," the concierge said teasingly. "It's not the end of the world. Why don't y'all go out on the town and have some fun? I'd be happy to set up a reservation at one of the finest restaurants Charleston has to offer."

It sounded good to us. S.B., Stryker, Zion, Cranny, Shakespeare, the Chief and I decided to go out.

We went to our rooms to change our clothes for the evening. S.B. was ready before I was and returned to the lobby without me.

When I followed, I glanced around to find her. Instead, I saw Mac, sitting on a sofa with Melinda, Miss Jewel's daughter. I was surprised by what Mac was doing — autographing what looked to be about 50 baseballs.

I couldn't believe it. Players signed that many baseballs when they wanted to make a little money on the side by exploiting their celebrity. Mac didn't grant interviews, acted as though she never cared about her stardom, and yet here she was, cashing in.

S.B. emerged from the hotel's newsstand and joined me. I inclined my head in Mac's direction and said, "Would you look at that?"

"Look at what?"

"Mac. Is she signing for dollars, or what?"

"Smokey, for Christ's sake!" There was real anger in S.B.'s voice. "Do you know what she's doing? I just talked to her, which is more than you must have done. Miss Jewel's church is having a fund-raiser, and it's going to be dedicated to Miss Jewel, because of her hospital stay. Melinda asked

Mac to sign baseballs as prizes for the people who bring in the most donations. *That's* what Mac's doing — doing something for charity, doing something to help Miss Jewel, doing something that makes ballplayers seem like more than spoiled stars."

I was mortified by my mistake. "S.B., I'm sorry. I didn't know. I feel stupid. But I don't know how to fix it."

"You can clean up your act, Smokey. You can goddamn clean up your act."

S.B. put her hand on the back of my neck and walked us over to Mac. I was scared to death, but I didn't dare protest.

"Hello, Melinda. Hey, Mac," S.B. said genially. "You want Smokey to sign some of those baseballs? They'd be real collectors' items."

"Better not. If both of our signatures were on there, people would figure at least one was forged," Mac said, but she was laughing, and we all laughed with her. Especially me.

Mac signed the last baseball. Melinda gathered them up with profuse thanks and with a shy good-bye, left us.

"Listen, Mac," S.B. said, "a bunch of us are going out to dinner — Smokey, me, Shakespeare, Cranny, Zion, Stryker and the Chief. Why don't you come, too?"

I could feel the pressure from S.B. beating down on me like the wings of an avenging angel. She was giving me a chance to redeem myself, and I didn't want to blow it.

"Come on, Mac. It'll be fun," I said, without choking.

Mac looked at S.B. She looked at me, suspiciously. She looked back at S.B., whose demeanor was as innocent as a saint's. Mac trusted S.B., so she said, "Okay."

Mac said she had some telephone calls to make and would meet us at the restaurant. She walked quickly, animatedly, toward the elevators.

I sat on the sofa and said contritely, "S.B., don't be mad at me. Please."

S.B. folded her arms and shook her head. "You are often a little ass, but it is curable."

We piled into two taxis and drove to the Wine Cellar, a premier restaurant at the Charleston waterfront. Once it had been a warehouse, but now its faded bricks and arched entryways housed an establishment that offered a seven-course dinner and the best wine list in the state. The concierge at the hotel had told us that we could expect to spend a genteelly paced three hours enjoying food and drink.

I sat next to Stryker and across from S.B. and flipped open my menu. Zion was already looking at hers, and she said, "Somehow I don't think our meal money is going to cover this."

"That's okay," Cranny said. "S.B. is going to pay for the extra out of her bonus money for the series she had against the Indies. Right, S.B.?"

"I don't have any bonus clauses in my contract," S.B. said.

"You don't? You play this game because you love it so much?" Cranny said.

"That's right. Don't you?"

"Well, I like my paycheck," Cranny said, a little defensively, and became engrossed in her menu.

"Did anybody else have the Sports News Network on this afternoon?" Shakespeare said. "Cranny and I were watching, and they said there was a big fight in the Goldrushers' clubhouse in Sacramento."

"Imagine that!" Cranny said, pinching her words and looking prissy. "Ladies, fighting in the clubhouse!"

"What was it about?" Stryker asked.

Shakespeare shrugged. "Don't know. Somebody from the team said it was a private matter — quote, unrelated to baseball, unquote."

"I bet I know," Zion said. "Was Wanda Klein in it?"

"As a matter of fact, she was," Shakespeare said. "How did you know that?"

"I didn't. I was just guessing," Zion said. "Wanda pitched on my college team. She had this one little failing. She was always going after somebody's lover. We used to call her Calendar, because all she was interested in was everybody else's dates."

"So you think she was coming on to somebody's honey?" Cranny asked.

"I'd bet on it," Zion said.

"Anybody get hurt?" Stryker asked.

She never got her question answered. There was a stir in the dining room. Mac had come in.

Sometimes you can become so familiar with someone that you forget to see her as others do. Sometimes it takes a new setting to see it again. Sometimes it takes a glass or two of wine. Put them both together, and you can have one of those moments.

Mac wasn't just Mac when she came in. She was *Mac MacDonnell,* and even if you had lived inside a box for the last ten years, you would have known that someone special was in your midst.

Mac, lithe and lean, had the carriage of a champion. Her features were composed and introspective, the countenance of an athlete who was used to being watched and rarely found wanting. Her face was marked only by the deep lines of concentration around her eyes, where she had narrowed her gaze under countless summer suns and stared down shattered pitchers.

When we had entered the restaurant, there had been a polite acknowledgment from the maitre d' and some inquisitive glances from the other patrons.

When Mac shook the rain from her hair and walked across the room, every diner and every waiter paid attention, offering homage once again to the Olympian hero whose home run had been a shot heard 'round the world.

She came to our table, sitting at the opposite end from me. The maitre d' solicitously opened a menu for her, and the wine steward filled her glass with a flourish. The waiter promised to take her order as soon as she was ready.

"What's good?" Mac asked us, as her new coterie of attendants withdrew respectfully.

"The wine is," I said.

"O'Neill, I thought your expertise was in *sour* grapes," Mac said.

My teammates laughed, and I simply shut up. I

was feeling too guilty about misunderstanding Mac's motives earlier to have any heart for a comeback.

Our appetizers came with more wine, and our soup came with more wine, and a fish course came with more wine, and then our entrees came with more wine. For a kid who had scraped to get by, I was eating the best meal of my life, and we still had salad, dessert and cheese yet to be served.

As the wine and the food made us mellow, our talk turned as always to baseball, the tree of life that sustained us.

"Does anybody know if it's raining in Boston?" Stryker asked. Boston and Indianapolis were scheduled to start a four-game series there.

"I think they're playing. The storm's coming from the south," Shakespeare said.

"I wonder who's going to win that series. We kicked butt against both of those teams and left them whimpering," Cranny said.

"Lorraine of Terror should be pitching tonight. I'd never bet against her, anymore than I'd bet against the Chief here," I said.

The Chief nodded her thanks at me. She hadn't said a word all evening, except to order her dinner.

"Hey, Chief, what makes you so blabby?" Shakespeare said.

"Must be the wine," the Chief said, deadpan, and we laughed.

"So, Smokey," Zion said. "Who's got the better team, Boston or us?"

"Without a doubt, we do. You know, even when the Colonials were winning last year, they were looking over their shoulders. The day they clinched, I can remember everyone sitting around the clubhouse saying they'd done it because a bunch of players had career years, and they didn't know whether they'd be able to do it again. Especially if Mac MacDonnell still had it."

Seduced by the wine, I had blurted out the truth. There was a moment of uncomfortable silence, and I shut my eyes briefly and wished I could disappear. I hadn't meant to chafe her.

From across the table, Mac was looking at me steadily, keeping her reaction to herself.

Then S.B. said softly, "Say, Mac, which is tougher: winning the Olympics or winning the division?"

"No question, winning the division," Mac said, a haunted note in her voice. "The Olympics is a rush. It's all adrenaline and instinct, and anyway, you're young and you think pressure means getting to practice on time. It's over almost before you realize you're there, and later you look at the videos and wonder whether they really happened."

Mac was still looking at me as she talked. I looked back, our eyes caught in a lock.

"Winning the division is grind-it-out guts, finding out day after day what you're made of. If you can get into the rhythm of it, if you can have a series like S.B. had against the Indies, you can feel like you're flying. Like you can do anything." Mac stared into her wine glass. We waited for what more she had to say, mesmerized by her oral reverie. "But it may not be there every day. It can come and go like a faithless lover, when the gods of baseball spurn your offerings and your most constant coach is time."

"Mac," S.B. implored, but Mac said nothing more.

"I have something to say." Shakespeare rose

unsteadily to her feet and peered at us with drunken earnestness. First, a toast. To the Delaware Blue Diamonds." We drank, not that any of us needed any more. "Second, a toast to Miss Jewel."

We drank again, with wordless murmurs of sympathy.

Then Shakespeare showed us how she had earned her nickname. "Finally, I give you *Henry V.* You must forgive the sexism of it. It was written a long, long time ago, but the sentiment is right."

She recited:

From this day to the ending of the world,
But we in it shall be remembered;
We few, we happy few, we band of brothers.

I was very drunk. Everything I saw was encircled by an out-of-focus, rose-colored halo, and in the center of it I was seeing Mac. She looked hard at me, and, I think, as Shakespeare's recitation went on, that Mac dipped the rim of her wine glass at me very slightly; but I was drunk and couldn't tell for sure.

For he, today, that sheds his blood with me,
Shall be my brother; be he ne'er so vile,
This day shall gentle his condition:
And gentlemen in safe homes now abed,
Shall think themselves accurs'd that were not
  here;
And hold their manhoods cheap, while any
  speaks
That fought with us upon Saint Crispin's Day.

It was a moment you wanted to go on forever, being with people you cared about, and knowing they cared about you, and knowing this moment would be the one you wanted to come back to you to cherish on the day you died. And did Mac dip her glass at me or not?

Somehow we got our check and settled our bill. I'm not sure how much it was, but S.B. kept telling me to take more money out of my wallet. I was beyond being able to figure it out for myself.

The rain had stopped. We called for taxis. I found myself crunched in a back seat with S.B. on my left and Mac on my right and started yelping.

"S.B.! That's my throwing hand you're squishing!"

"Nobody cares about your throwing hand. You play first base. Just worry about your glove hand."

"Oh."

S.B. reached across my shoulders to touch Mac.

"It's okay, S.B. I'm all right," Mac said. They shared a smile of friendship that I had no business witnessing, and we rode with S.B.'s hand on Mac's shoulder, and me pressed between them.

The wine was still building in my head like a fatal dose of poison. When we were dropped off, I made it out of the taxi, but then the hotel started rolling like the picture on a television set without a vertical hold.

"S.B.!" I said.

I was swaying. S.B. steadied me and said, "Mac, give me a hand, will you?"

"Goddamn it," Mac said, but she came to help. They each took an arm as we walked inside. Frankly, they weren't a heck of a lot more stable than I was.

"If Lefevre catches us, all three of our butts are going to be on the bench tomorrow," Mac said.

But Lefevre wasn't there, and we managed our way to the room I shared with S.B.

"What now?" Mac asked.

"Help me get her to bed," S.B. said.

They stripped off my clothes, not very gently, and dumped me between the sheets.

"Christ, don't light a match if she exhales," Mac said. "The fumes'll catch fire."

"If she croaks tonight, she won't need any embalming fluid. She's pickled enough," S.B. said.

I opened my eyes, with great effort. "Fuck you both," I said.

"Ornery little shit," Mac said.

"A first-class bastard," S.B. said.

"No fucking gratitude," Mac said.

Their voices were softened and husky from the wine and somehow soothing. I suppose their obscenity-laced conversation continued, but I fell asleep.

CHAPTER ELEVEN

The problem with me is, no matter how tired, sick or hungover I am, I still wake up early. The late summer's pale mist of daylight was just washing into the room when I came to, wondering why I was feeling as though someone had put a ball and chain on my ankle and pitched me overboard into the sea.

My lungs hurt, my head ached, and my body was splayed out and sweating. For someone accustomed to embracing each new day like a blessing, this was not good.

Then I remembered and decided it was worth feeling this way. We'd had a good time, we Blue Diamonds, and Shakespeare's poetry had been sublime, and S.B. and Mac had put me to bed, and didn't I have some recollection of Mac dipping her wine glass in a bare salute? I wasn't sure. I *was* sure of the obscenities they'd crooned as I sputtered out and went to sleep.

I had to have some Alka-Seltzer. Advanced formula, if possible. S.B. was still asleep. I found a sweatshirt and shorts and lumbered toward the lobby.

I got there just as Coach Lefevre was leaving the hotel shop with the daily newspapers. There was no escaping her. I was trapped as helplessly as a ballplayer in a rundown.

"Good morning, O'Neill," Lefevre said. Then she got a better look at me and saw the shape I was in. "What were you doing last night?"

"Drinking, Coach. Heavily."

Lefevre came up close and tough like a drill sergeant. If she thought she could intimidate me, she was certainly right.

"What's the rule, O'Neill?"

"Don't drink so much that it makes you sick."

"And what did you do?"

"Drank enough to get sick."

"Who else was with you? Or am I supposed to believe it was just you and a bottle?"

"Me and several bottles," I said. If I went down, I wasn't taking anyone with me, although there was a certain temptation to name Mac. Lefevre wouldn't have believed it, anyway.

She studied me with scientific interest, as she had the day she took the check for five hundred dollars from me. "I've been a coach for a lot of years, but there's one lesson I can't seem to learn. Whenever I let somebody off, she always does something worse. I shouldn't have let you go when I caught you with the booze on the bus leaving Boston. O'Neill, you can count on Mulligan starting at first base today. Any questions?"

"Yes, Coach. Did you happen to notice whether the hotel store had any advanced-formula Alka-Seltzer?"

I thought I saw a flicker of laughter in Lefevre's eyes, but she doused it very quickly. She was a pro. "I did not, O'Neill. You'll have to check for yourself," she said and let me go.

I was furious over Lefevre's decision to put Mulligan in the lineup, but I was damned if I'd let her know it. I bought my Alka-Seltzer and returned to the room.

S.B. was stirring, and she didn't seem to be much better off than I was. "What do you have there? Alka-Seltzer? Fix me one, too, okay?"

I did and handed it to her as she propped herself against the headboard of the bed. "Cheers," I said, and we clinked glasses.

S.B. looked wan, with dark and deep half-circles beneath her eyes. A blood vessel twitched in her temple. "I feel like hell," she said unnecessarily.

"You don't feel as bad as I do. I ran into Lefevre. She's benching me."

I picked up a pillow from the other bed and slammed it down on the mattress. I knocked dirty clothes from a chair. I kicked a trash can. I entertained S.B. with a repertoire of obscenities usually reserved for umpires and sportswriters.

"Don't keep it inside. Let your emotions go," S.B. said drily.

"Hell, S.B., I hate to sit."

"I know, Smokey. It's real tough luck. Come on, let's order room service and try to get rid of these hangovers. I'm taking the hint from what happened to you. I'm not leaving here until I look like I could do a commercial for drinking milk."

I got a smirk from Cranny and a sympathetic pat on the back from Zion when they saw the lineup for the game. Lefevre told inquiring sportswriters that I had earned a day off.

"I earned it all right," I grumbled to S.B. "I earned it by being in the wrong place at the wrong time."

I slouched on the bench with the pitchers, sitting between the Chief and Stryker, and fidgeted while the play on the field went to hell.

One of the reasons that Lefevre had traded for me was that the Blue Diamonds needed a leadoff hitter. Marcia Chang had done the job, and although she was usually a tough out at the plate, she hated it. You have to be a little bit of a showboat to hit first, and that wasn't Marcia's style.

Now she was out there again, and suffering. All she wanted to do was to get her at-bats over with. Unluckily for her, the Charleston Rebels were starting Bonnie Leigh Lousma that day, a pitcher with the widest blue eyes I'd ever seen and the patience to let Marcia get herself out. Which she did.

Marcia uncharacteristically carried her discomfort at the plate into right field, and in the fourth inning she let a ball drop in front of her for a base hit. The runner stole second, and the Rebels had a player in scoring position.

The next batter hit the ball sharply to the right side of the infield, and I like to think it was one I would have fielded. It skipped by Mulligan, playing in my place, for a single and an RBI, and the Rebels were on their way to a five-run inning.

The Blue Diamonds were hitting but not bunching anything. We stranded more bodies than a shipwreck on a desert island. The only offensive success belonged to Mulligan, who clubbed two solo home runs. We lost, 7–2.

I had mixed feelings about it, but mostly I was frustrated by the loss and embarrassed that I had contributed to it by getting myself benched.

Afterwards, Lefevre pulled me aside. I don't know quite what I expected, but it sure wasn't what she said. "I'm going with the hot bat," Lefevre told me. "Mulligan deserves another start tomorrow."

I knew I should keep my mouth shut, but I hadn't felt so aggrieved since I had played for Coach Pettibone. The next thing I knew, I was saying insolently, "Coach, are you trying to teach me a lesson?"

Pettibone would have benched me for the rest of the season. Heck, Pettibone would have traded me to a team that thought of me as Public Enemy Number One. Which she did.

But Lefevre was not Pettibone. She chuckled. "Smokey O," she said, "people like you don't learn lessons this way. It only makes you balky. I am doing what I said I was doing — rewarding a player who came off the bench for me and did the job.

"You won't die, sitting down another day. You used to be platooned in Boston, as I recall. Don't worry. I am still a card-carrying member of the Smokey O Admiration Society." Lefevre put her arm around me, and damned if she didn't kiss me on the forehead.

"For crying out loud, Coach," I said, "how am I supposed to be mad at you when you treat me like this?"

Lefevre laughed. I laughed. And I knew why she was called the best coach that ever put on a uniform and captained a team through the press of competition, with a touch that was gentle and sure and true.

All things considered, I wasn't in too bad a mood when the next game started. The Chief was pitching, so it figured to be a good one to watch. I sat next to Stryker, pulled my cap brim low and tilted my head back against the dugout wall.

The Blue Diamonds went hitless in the first inning, and so did the Rebels. The game was shaping up as a pitching duel. I saw Lefevre glance at me. She must have been thinking the same thing that I was. If this was to be a low-scoring game, she'd be better off with my glove in the field to make the defensive plays.

But it wasn't my problem.

The teams still were scoreless after six innings. Mac came in from center field and surprised me by tossing her glove into my lap. "Do something useful," she needled. "Caddy for me."

I was furious. I held her glove while the Blue Diamonds batted, still unable to put any runs on the scoreboard, then I stood up and pressed close to her to return it.

"I hope you rot in hell," I told her, softly so no one else could hear.

"Better than rotting on the bench," she said.

The Charleston fans stood for the seventh-inning stretch. They were looking for luck and they got it — and at what a cost to the Blue Diamonds.

Bertie Smith, the Rebels' muscular right fielder, led off with a cheap infield hit. She advanced to second base on a fielder's choice.

The next batter hit a slow bounder toward right, just out of Mulligan's reach, with Bertie getting a good jump and streaking for third. Marcia Chang charged in from right field to pick up the ball, while Bertie rounded third and headed for home.

Marcia gloved the ball on an in-between hop, which is why she hesitated just a fraction before throwing and why Cranny in her catching gear was as outstretched as she could be when the ball and Bertie arrived simultaneously.

Cranny was big, but Bertie was bigger. Bertie crashed into Cranny, who went down on her back as fiercely as a tree felled by a lumberjack. The ball trickled away.

Cranny did not get up. The Chief, who was backing up the play, threw the ball to Shakespeare at third base to hold the runner, then went down on her knees next to Cranny.

"What's wrong?" the Chief cried. "Cranny, what's wrong?"

Cranny beat against the turf with her glove and gasped. Shakespeare sprinted in from third. Lefevre and the medical personnel raced toward her.

"My back," Cranny said in breathless pain. "My back."

She couldn't rise. We watched in fright as Cranny left the field on a stretcher. Bertie ran beside to apologize, but no one was blaming her. It wasn't a cheap shot; it was just bad timing.

Lefevre sent in Tina Corrozi, the backup catcher, and the Chief returned to the mound. But it wasn't any good. Without Cranny, the Chief's rhythm was gone.

She got shelled. The Rebels batted around, scoring four runs. Bertie Smith made the last out.

It didn't help that Mulligan failed to scoop out a low throw from Gonzales at shortstop. When the Blue Diamonds took the field again, Lefevre sent me in to play first.

Not that it mattered. The Rebels were rolling and beat us 7–1. Shakespeare accounted for our lone run by clouting a meaningless homer in the top of the ninth.

Meanwhile, Boston had taken two games from Indianapolis. The Blue Diamonds and the Colonials were tied for first place, only this time they were on the way up and we were on the way down.

Lefevre, Shakespeare and S.B. dressed quickly after the game and left for the hospital to be with

Cranny. The rest of us boarded the team bus for the hotel.

I commandeered the last seat, where Shakespeare and Cranny usually sat. I fretted about Cranny and, despite my best intentions, nursed my wounded feelings over not starting.

We straggled into the hotel in ones and twos, looking nothing like a team. Was it only two nights ago that I had dined in bliss at the Wine Cellar? The Southern charm of this town was wearing off fast.

I went to my room. I was flipping through a magazine with explicit pictures in it when the telephone rang.

"Smokey O?" said a honeyed voice that I would recognize anywhere.

"Clarabelle? What are you calling for? Where are you?"

"I'm in the lobby. Come down and have a drink with me."

"When did you get here? I didn't see your Mercedes parked outside."

"I just got here. I flew in and rented a Jaguar."

"I should have guessed. What are you doing here?"

"Come down and I'll tell you."

I was as suspicious as I could be. Clarabelle was not exactly the bluebird of happiness when she flew in someplace, but more like the angel of death. It was a cinch she hadn't come because she admired my sexual technique.

I took a second to brush my hair and then caught the elevator to the lobby.

Clarabelle was standing in the center like a sun goddess, her tawny hair shining in the muted light of the lamp globes. She was wearing a dark green jumpsuit, neckline plunging, and the green scarf that had driven me wild was knotted around her throat. Everyone in the lobby was watching her, either stealing glances or simply staring.

"Smokey O," she said, lifting an eyebrow at me. "Let's go into the bar. I'm parched from travel."

The hotel lounge was called Charleston Charlie's, a cavelike place that affected a sense of tawdriness, with satin pillows and trimmings of red and gold. We sat at the polished, darkly gleaming bar on tall pillowed stools.

"What will you have?" Clarabelle asked me when the bartender appeared.

"Ginger ale," I told the bartender, "and leave the bottle on the bar, please." I'd had enough alcohol earlier in the week to last me, and anyway, if Lefevre came by after going to the hospital, I didn't want her to see me sucking down more booze.

Clarabelle ordered a Beefeater's gin and tonic, then said, "What's the matter, Smokey? On the wagon?"

"No. Just not in the mood."

"You don't have a substance-abuse problem, do you?"

"I do not. Write it, and I swear I'll sue you from here to hell and back."

"My, you are testy this evening." She flipped open her notepad. "Could it be because you've been benched?"

I glared. "I played today."

"A late-inning defensive replacement. A *very* late-inning defensive replacement."

"Is this what you came to Charleston for? To find out why I was sitting?"

"As a matter of fact, Smokey, it is. *Sports Illustrated* has invested much time and money in my story about the Delaware Blue Diamonds. It is scheduled to run in two weeks, which is the next time you play the Boston Colonials. If you're not starting anymore, I've got some rewriting to do."

"I'm starting," I said, spitting out the words as though I'd gotten a mouthful of poisoned food.

I hoped I was starting. Because of Cranny's injury, I hadn't had a chance to see Lefevre after the game. But I had to be. Lefevre had said she was still a "card-carrying member of the Smokey O Admiration Society," hadn't she?

"Why didn't you start the last two games?" Clarabelle said.

She never got an answer. I stopped talking as we spied Mac coming into the bar with Stryker.

Mac spotted us, perched like a couple of rival falcons on our stools, and left Stryker standing in the doorway to come over. She leaned on the bar next to Clarabelle and gave us the look of a cop who's seen two notorious crooks in a church pew and can't do a thing about it.

"Hello, Claire," Mac said.

"Hello, Jill," Clarabelle said.

"I thought you two knew enough to stay away from each other."

"I'm doing an interview, Jill. I make my living as a writer, you know."

"You make your living as a character assassin."

"My, everybody's testy this evening. I am here merely to discover why Smokey O is sitting on the bench. Perhaps you know?"

"Sure," Mac said. "O'Neill is on the bench because that's where Coach Lefevre figures she can contribute the most."

I'd had it. "I'll tell you what, Mac. You may have something there, because I've had as many RBIs on the bench in the last two games as you've had at the plate."

Mac's eyes were molten. I'll never know what she wanted to say to me, because she saw Clarabelle's pen gliding on her notepad. Instead, Mac said, "Goddamn you, Claire," and stalked away.

"Hey, you're not writing this stuff, are you?" I said.

Clarabelle smiled so sweetly. "I don't recall hearing those three magic little words: Off the record."

I slid off the bar stool. "You are low," I snapped and left her.

"I suppose," Clarabelle called after me, "that this means we're not having another drink?"

CHAPTER TWELVE

"Cranny's going to be okay," S.B. said when she came in, the relief in her voice as pure as rainwater. "She's hurting, and she's having back spasms, but she's all right. The doctors say she's day-to-day and could be back anytime."

"That is better news than I expected," I said.

We needed Cranny's bat and we needed Cranny's humor, but mostly we needed her mind behind the plate, clicking along as efficiently as the beads on an abacus, and we needed her easy touch with the pitchers.

"She's going to stay in the hospital overnight, but she'll fly out with us after the game tomorrow."

"Good. It sure looked a lot worse than that when she went down."

"Meanwhile," S.B. said, giving me one of those very pointed looks in which she had nevertheless already forgiven me my trespasses, "I leave you alone for a few hours and I hear you're stirring up trouble again."

I winced. "How did you find out?"

"I ran into Stryker on my way in."

"The snitch."

"Don't blame her. I saw her sitting in the lobby and wondered why she was staying up past her bedtime."

Stryker was a notorious early-to-bed type. When she talked about having trouble staying awake for the nightly news, she didn't mean the eleven o'clock edition. She meant the six-thirty show. If a night game went into extra innings and she had to pitch, there were usually a lot of jokes about stoking her with coffee.

"So what was Sleepy doing? Waiting for Snow White and the rest of the dwarfs?"

"Not exactly," S.B. said drily. "She was waiting for Mac, who, Stryker said, had followed Clarabelle out of the hotel sometime before."

"I didn't know that part," I said, then told S.B. my version of the story.

"Smokey, for God's sake, what are we going to do? I thought you and Mac had declared a truce, and now this happens."

"Goddamn it, S.B., it's not my fault. I was sitting there having a drink — having a *ginger ale* — with Clarabelle when Mac came over and started it."

"But Smokey, you *know* about Clarabelle. She's one of those people who just can't bear happy endings. What do you suppose the odds are that she invited you down and then called Mac so that you two could have a 'chance' meeting and mix it up?"

"Oh God, S.B., suppose you're right? I swear, that Clarabelle is a fucking spider. I can't believe I was so stupid. I've got the brains of a hot-water bottle."

S.B. tried not to laugh, but she couldn't help herself. "The problem with you, Smokey, is that you never own up to your mistakes, you know what I mean?"

"I wish I had fewer mistakes to own up to. I can guarantee you that I'll steer clear of Clarabelle from now on, but I doubt she'll come around again. I think she's got her story, and got it good."

S.B. nodded. "But it's not just your fault, Smokey. I don't understand Mac. She should have walked out of the bar as soon as she saw you and Clarabelle talking."

"And you say Mac's gone after her?"

"That's what Stryker said. You tell me, Smokey, what's Clarabelle got, anyway?"

I blushed.

"Hey, I nearly forgot," S.B. said. "Lefevre asked me to tell you that you're starting tomorrow. She said she's sorry she didn't have the chance to say so herself."

I nodded, more grateful and relieved than I cared to let on.

"So be ready. We need you to be perking if we're

going to salvage one game from this God-awful series."

I came out smoking, banged a triple for my first at-bat. S.B. walked, and it looked as though we were on our way to a big inning.

But Mac went down on a foul pop, and Shakespeare hit into a double play. I was the last runner who got as far as third base. We lost, 2–0, swept by the Charleston Rebels. They hooted and high-fived as though the Jubilee had arrived.

Up in Boston, the Colonials won. The Delaware Blue Diamonds were two games out of first place and starting to breathe hard.

"I just want to get out of this town," I moaned to S.B. as we dressed after the game.

"This is the way we were feeling before you got here — just not clicking and not being able to figure out why. We'll turn it around," S.B. said.

A bunch of other players — Gonzales, Zion, the Chief, Mulligan and Marcia Chang — were attracted to the unruffled tone in S.B.'s voice and gathered to listen.

"Every season has its peaks and valleys," S.B. said. "We had one of those peaks to get us into first place. It's natural to fall off a little, but believe me, we'll come back stronger and surge further. Anyway, Boston just isn't as good as we are."

"Got to start scrapping again. Got to be the junkyard dogs again," Zion said.

"We need Cranny for that. We need Miss Jewel, too," Gonzales said.

"They'll be back," S.B. said.

Most of the Blue Diamonds were listening now and feeling better — except for Mac, who was off by herself and brooding. The bolts and tracers that normally flew from her bat had vanished, and its barrenness left her cheerless and unhearing.

Mac had gotten to me with her crack about caddying for her, but I knew I had gotten to her more when I had insulted her in front of Clarabelle. My time on the bench was a fluke, as we both knew; but the ever-present Greek chorus of sportswriters had already resumed the chant of wondering whether Mac's stardom was flaming out.

Mac sat by herself on the bus when we left the ballpark and did not bother to join in the joyful noise that greeted Cranny at the airport. She even shrugged away the gentle hand that Lefevre laid on her shoulder.

Her torment continued during our last stop on the road trip, when we played the Nashville Stars, the perennial division losers. The Blue Diamonds did all right, winning the first game, dropping the second and winning the third. It kept us two games in back of Boston, which won two out of three in its series with the New York Aces.

Mac's bat, however, remained impotent. She spoke little, although she was polite — even to me. When I crossed the plate with the go-ahead run in the first game, driven in by S.B.'s faultless suicide-squeeze bunt, Mac was there to greet me.

But her eyes were as opaque as prison windows, and her handshake was as impersonal as an undertaker's.

The sportswriters, harpies now, were merciless. One Nashville headline writer contorted Mac's miseries into this: "Mac MacDonnell: From Might to Mite?"

It was a relief to return to the friendly confines of Du Pont Stadium, where the home team was the good guys who always wore white. Our first opponents were the New York Aces, who flew in from Boston to play us.

There is something about New York that Delaware loves to hate. Maybe it's just a natural misfit because of size. Maybe it's that New Yorkers think no one is as sophisticated as they are, and Delawareans know that New Yorkers think it.

Whatever the reason, the Blue Diamonds understood instinctively why Tug McGraw, the Phillies' relief pitcher, celebrated Philadelphia's World Series triumph in 1980 by screaming, "New York City can take this world championship and stick it!"

The Aces were a perfect foil for us. We pummeled them in the first game, slipped by them in the second and fought them to a snarling standstill in the third, finally winning in the twelfth inning when Gonzales improbably stole home.

It should have been enough for us, but we were more morose than merry, because up in Boston, the Colonials swept the hapless Nashville Stars. Despite our best efforts, Boston had us locked in the dungeon of second place.

And Mac still wasn't hitting.

The Indianapolis Indies came to town for a

four-game series, determined to pay us back for what we had done to them in their ballpark, when S.B. had that dream series.

The Indies took the first three games from us. Fortunately, the Charleston Rebels were doing the same thing to the Boston Colonials, so we didn't lose any more ground in the standings. For us, there was relief. For Boston, there was excruciating frustration as they watched us lose without getting buried.

We probably would have lost the fourth game to the Indies, too, if it hadn't been for Zion.

On the morning before the final game, Zion was scheduled to run a baseball clinic for Little League-age children in Wilmington. She asked some of us to go with her.

I rode up with Zion, S.B., Stryker and Mac, but the best news was that Cranny was going, too. The doctors finally had cleared her to play again.

We drove to the Judy Johnson baseball field at Second and Du Pont Streets. It was named for William Julius "Judy" Johnson, a star third base player in the old Negro Leagues and the first Delawarean enshrined in the Hall of Fame. Every inner-city kid who could walk, bike, hop a bus or cadge a ride seemed to be at that park, waiting for us.

The kids were too excited to listen, so Zion declared open season on autographs until they settled down. We signed baseballs, gloves, scraps of paper, T-shirts, photos clipped from newspapers — anything they thrust at us.

Zion finally got the clinic going. She was the ringmaster, and we were the performers amidst dozens and dozens of tiny, happy-go-lucky baseball players with miniature mitts and oversized batting helmets and a colorful array of T-shirts, usually with the insignia of either the Philadelphia Phillies or the Delaware Blue Diamonds on them.

S.B. talked about how to play the infield. Mac spoke about the outfield. I demonstrated running the bases, stealing and sliding. Stryker gave pointers on pitching.

The kids were enthusiastic, but they saved their biggest cheers for Cranny. This baseball-crazy crowd knew she was just coming off the disabled list, and they shouted joyously as Cranny wiggled, mugged and moaned her way into a catcher's crouch to show off the tools of ignorance.

We were laughing, too.

For the *pièce de résistance*, Zion asked Cranny and me to hit against Stryker.

"She'll be throwing for real," Zion said, as Stryker toed the pitcher's mound and smirked at us.

"Oh, God," groaned Cranny.

"She'll make fools of us," I said.

"That's the idea," Zion said.

We were nothing if not good sports. Cranny pulled seniority on me, so I had to go first.

The kids filled the bleachers. They were attentive but fidgety and looked like hyperkinetic ants. Zion chose some of the more coordinated of them and sent them out to play the field — in the unlikely event that Cranny or I hit anything.

I went to the plate, and Zion took the umpire's spot to call balls and strikes.

"Swing at everything," Stryker called to me. "I'm just throwing strikes."

"Big clue. That's all you ever throw," I grumbled. I hadn't been on the receiving end of Stryker's pitching since I left the Boston Colonials, and I knew I wasn't up to hitting the stuff that she had.

In came the first offering — a fastball that had more action to it than a bump-and-grind strip tease. I whiffed obligingly as the kids squealed with delight. I counted myself lucky to foul off the second fastball, then came up with a clean miss on a slider that radar couldn't have followed.

"Strike three! You're out!" said Zion, as if everyone in the ballpark didn't already know it. I dragged off.

Cranny made the sign of the cross before settling herself in the batter's box, but it didn't help. She didn't do any better than I did — two fastballs and a slider and she was gone. Stryker blew her a kiss.

Zion stood in front of the plate. "Okay, kids, that ends it — unless you want to see Mac hit," she said.

The little fans went bonkers. Out of their mindless screaming and jumping, there emerged a heartfelt chorus: "We want Mac! We want Mac! We want Mac!"

Mac strolled to the plate, as easy as a schoolgirl on the first day of summer vacation. She didn't seem to care at all that it was Stryker out there.

Maybe Stryker never intended to throw Mac her real stuff. Maybe Mac's posture persuaded her. Whatever the reason, I saw her smiling at Mac and sensed the batting-practice pitches coming.

Zion did, too. She gestured her impromptu fielders backwards. "Sink out," she said. They took a few steps toward the fences and stopped. "Sink way out," she said, and they backed up a little farther; but I knew and the rest of the Blue Diamonds knew it would never be far enough.

Stryker laid the first pitch in there. Mac's muscles rippled, and the ball arced in an electric charge across the cadmium sky, so high that the little fielders simply gaped at it as it ripped beyond the perimeter of the field.

Then they sat down. No one told them to; they simply did it, somehow knowing that their presence was no longer required.

Stryker served up the pitches, and Mac rocked into a state of primal rhythm and finesse. From her bat shot fireworks and lightning bolts, shooting stars and flaring rockets — a circus of brilliance that dazzled the children who had never seen it before and us who thought we had seen it all.

When Mac finally held up her hand to say she was finished, the kids swarmed her from the bleachers, and she lowered herself laughing to the sweet-smelling turf and was lost among them like Gulliver amidst the Lilliputians.

A toddler, someone's younger sister, made it to the center of the heap and sat soberly on Mac's chest, her grave brown eyes staring at Mac's face.

Pinned down by the child, Mac reached out and tickled the youngsters who sported like puppies around her and ruffled their hair. We had never seen her so unburdened and free.

Children have a lot of energy, but never much at one time, and by and by they became exhausted and drifted away. The last to leave was the toddler, when someone took her by the hand and drew her off Mac's chest.

Zion, Stryker, Cranny, S.B. and I looked down wonderingly at the grass-stained hero, still prone on the field.

"What the hell was that?" Cranny said.

"I had almost forgotten," Mac said, "how much fun this game can be."

CHAPTER THIRTEEN

The Indianapolis Indies never knew what hit them. S.B. and I grounded out without a fuss when we led off the last game of the series. Then Mac walked slowly to the plate, her head down.

Bobbie Allen, the Indies pitcher, winked at her catcher and jauntily adjusted her cap. She was sure she was encountering a slumping team, with Mac the most slump-ridden of us all.

But I knew why Mac's head was down. She was remembering the feel of the bat and the swarm of children just hours ago at the Judy Johnson baseball field, and she was afloat on the talent rising within her like an answered prayer.

S.B. nudged me with her elbow as she sat beside me on the dugout bench. "I wouldn't want to be Bobbie Allen right now," she said.

"Neither would I."

Bobbie Allen kissed the outside of the plate with a fastball, but it was a kiss of death. Mac's shoulders hitched, and she hit a screaming banshee of a shot that missed clearing the right field fence by about a foot. Mac sprinted into second base with a stand-up double, and Bobbie Allen stood on the mound shaking.

Shakespeare singled Mac home, and the Blue Diamonds turned into a wrecking crew. We smashed the Indies 7–2. Mac finished up with two doubles and a home run, and the fans hollered themselves hoarse for her.

We bounded into the clubhouse after the last sullen Indianapolis player was out, and surprise, surprise, Miss Jewel was standing there like a magic charm to greet us. She was a little bit thinner and a little unsteady, but she caught Mac in a huge hug and held her dearly. We yelped and hugged Miss Jewel and one another, too. We were family again.

Miss Jewel said she wasn't allowed to work yet, but she could attend our games. She seemed a little sad about it, and we interrupted one another to protest earnestly that it was she we cared about, and not her work. Even if she was the best clubhouse manager that had ever drawn breath.

We did our post-game interviews quickly and kicked the sportswriters out, and then the horseplay began.

Shakespeare snapped a sopping towel against Cranny's broad butt, leaving a blushing welt, and Cranny whipped around and sprayed deodorant at Shakespeare.

The deodorant mist made Gonzales sneeze, so she retaliated by shaking up a can of soda and letting the foam fly at Shakespeare and Cranny. They grabbed soda cans and went after Gonzales.

Zion and Marcia Chang merrily rubbed shaving cream into Mulligan's red hair. For all I knew, they were preparing to shave it off. Mulligan was too humiliated to struggle, but she kept repeating, "Shit! Shit! Shit!"

I was helping the Chief stuff ice cubes inside Stryker's underwear as she squalled, when I was pulled away and slammed hard against the wall.

It was Mac, and she looked at me intensely and indecipherably as she held me there. I was scared.

"Up against the wall, motherfucker," she said, her fingers at my neck and the heels of her palms pressed against my collarbone.

"Mac, nice piece of hitting today," I said, trying to appease her.

Then Zion and Cranny flung themselves on Mac, wrestling her away from me. Mac rarely played, and they weren't about to let this opportunity go by.

"I'm not finished with you," Mac said to me, before putting up a fight and swearing liberally at Zion and Cranny.

They dragged her scuffling into the showers and turned the water on as cold as it would go. Mac gasped and swore some more and twisted mightily to free herelf, but Zion and Cranny had her good.

"Say uncle, you bastard," Cranny said.

"Uncle, you bastard!" Mac snarled.

"Say it nicely!" Cranny said, and she laced her fingers into Mac's hair and forced her head under the piercing cold water.

Mac sputtered and struggled. "Uncle!" she said. "Uncle!"

They let her go and retreated, laughing. Mac limply shut off the shower and stood there shivering.

I must say, I enjoyed it. The cold water had taken the fight out of her, and she didn't have the will to come after me again.

Like the children at the Judy Johnson ballpark, we spent our energy extravagantly and gave out.

Miss Jewel looked around and shook her head. There were soaking clothes and towels everywhere and spilled soda, empty soda cans, puddles of water and shriveling gobs of shaving cream.

"Girls, girls!" she said, with happiness and love stretching her smile wide. "Look at this mess! Just look at it! And I'm not allowed to clean it up!"

Well, someone would — but not us. We were ballplayers and we had something else on our minds.

Most of us went to the Deer Park tavern to celebrate, and when the drinking was done, not too many of us meant to go home alone.

From the Deer Park entryway, I called a Boston sportswriter who had seemed interested when I played for the Colonials. She was in town to write a feature on us before the big match-up between the two teams.

The sportswriter was willing, but she had a story to do and couldn't meet me at the tavern. She said to come by her motel room after she was off deadline.

I got a beer and sat down at a table with Shakespeare and Cranny, who were staring lasciviously into each other's eyes and whispering about what they wanted to do to each other once they were home. What I overheard was pretty spicy. I wondered why they had bothered to come to the Deer Park. Anticipation, I guess.

S.B. slid onto the bench next to me.

"What do you say, S.B.?" I said.

"I say I'm going to have a drink with you and then go romance that history professor I'm seeing. She had a class tonight, or she'd have come to the game." S.B. liked them intellectual.

"How's it going?"

"She's into American Studies this semester. Last time she told me about Martin Luther King before we got down to it. I think it's Watergate tonight."

"Why don't you come home with me, S.B.? I know who Richard Nixon was." I wasn't serious, and S.B. knew it.

"Sorry, Smokey, I room with you. Your body holds no mystery for me." We laughed, and then S.B. said smilingly, "Anyway, this friendship we have, there's nothing casual about it."

She tousled my hair. I was touched. "You've helped me survive, S.B."

She laughed. "The season's not over yet."

The feeling I had was too emotional to prolong. I escaped by drinking my beer.

"Come on, Smokey, walk out with me," S.B. said.

I checked my watch. It was almost time to see the Boston sportswriter. "Okay. I'm tired of watching Shakespeare and Cranny make eyes at each other, anyway."

I drove to the sportswriter's motel and rang up her room. She was there and invited me up.

We messed around, but it wasn't great sex.

Spare me from reporters. I think they'd rather write about it than do it.

Coach Lefevre called us together the next day, before the start of a three-game series against the Charleston Rebels.

The clubhouse had indeed been straightened up, as we knew it would be. Ball players possess a simple faith. We may outgrow our belief in Santa Claus, but we never stop trusting that someone will pick up after us.

At Lefevre's summons, we lounged on the clubhouse benches and against the lockers. We looked nothing like the disheveled mob that beat it out of there the day before. Instead, we wore our white home uniforms, cleaned and pressed, and we angled fresh blue baseball caps over our combed and styled hair.

"You all did a lot of celebrating last night," Lefevre said, a mocking tone to her voice. "You all did a lot of celebrating for a team that needed four tries before you finally took a game from a fifth-place club."

Hell, I thought, *this is not going to be fun.* I made the mistake of clearing my throat and attracting Lefevre's attention.

"O'Neill. You were having yourself a rip-roaring good time. Did you manage to behave yourself?"

"Unlikely that I'd say," I said mildly.

"O'Neill. And I thought you were one of those Girl Scout types, honest in thought, word and deed."

I shut up and waited for the snickers to die down.

"You've had your fun, people. Now it's time to get focused," Lefevre said. "Let's review where we are. Boston lost yesterday, so we're a game out of first. Boston got swept by the Charleston Rebels, who are coming in here now and hoping to sweep us again, they way they did it to us in their ballpark. They are making a habit of this. If the Rebels get any more sweeps, they're going to be doing broom commercials. They are making a damn fine run at knocking New York out of third place. I remind you of this because I figure you're all thinking about Boston coming in here after Charleston leaves. We can't afford to look beyond this series. We've got to focus on the Rebels now, or it won't matter a damn how we play Boston. After Boston, the season has two weeks left in it. We are at the nub of the matter right now. If we put it to Charleston, we control our own destiny when Boston comes to town. This is where we want to be. This is what we've been driving for."

Lefevre started walking among us. When she got to S.B., she put her hand on S.B.'s shoulder and said, "It's not supposed to be easy. We don't even want it to be easy. If we were leading a division of mediocre teams, no one would remember us. The Goldrushers are running away with it in the West, and who even cares? But everybody in the country is talking about this rivalry between Delaware and Boston, about two teams with a lot of heart taking it to each other. This is the way you want to be remembered. This is the story you want mothers and fathers to tell their kids when they teach them about baseball. This is what you were born for."

She paused. "Except for Mac. Mac, you were born for the Olympics. Unless you're ready to be born again."

We were startled by Lefevre's barb at Mac. We were startled whenever anyone dared disturb the peace of our moody and unpredictable center fielder. In apprehension, we looked at Mac. How would she react?

Mac was sitting by herself at the end of a bench. She was balancing a bat on her knee in her clean, white uniform, as though the bat were a lance held by a knight of yore.

She was laughing, and so we laughed too, in relief and confidence and in anticipation of what we would do to Charleston.

We took two out of three from the Rebels, and it wasn't easy. Boston also won two out of three.

The Delaware Blue Diamonds were still a game out of first, and it was showdown time.

CHAPTER FOURTEEN

On the morning we were to play Boston, when I came home from running, my telephone was ringing. I was surprised, because it was still very early. I had gone out at first light to avoid what promised to be a late summer hot spell, stuffy enough to leave you groggy.

It was Stryker on the line, and as soon as she said my name, I knew something was wrong. "Smokey, my God, have you seen *Sports Illustrated*?"

"No."

"Clarabelle's story is in there. You don't come out so good. Neither does Mac. Actually, none of us do."

"Fuck."

"We don't need this. We've got Boston coming in for three games."

"Yeah. Stryker, I'll get back to you. I've got to get a copy."

I was trembling. I got my car and headed for the newsstand near the Deer Park on Main Street. I drive a pretty flashy sports car, my one indulgence, and it usually gets me a look or two. Today I was grateful I had never ordered one of those personalized license plates, saying "SMOKEY" or "1 BASE" or something. I didn't want to be noticed any more than I had to be.

The clerk in the newsstand was setting up a display of *Sports Illustrated* in the window. It was as bad as it could be. The cover blared: "From Boston to Delaware, A Tale of Two Teams." The illustrator had drawn caricatures of Mac and me, standing back to back like duelists, pistols upraised in our hands.

I wished I had been wearing sunglasses and a hat, instead of standing there in nothing but a sweat-drenched T-shirt and shorts. The clerk looked at the magazine and at me and did a double-take.

"It's you!" the clerk said.

"No kidding." I left without waiting for my change.

I drove home, pulled down the shades and turned to Clarabelle's prose. It was so fine and seductive, a yarn of lies so entangling, so enticing, that I'd never get out of it, not if all the saints and angels in heaven testified on my behalf.

It began:

Mac MacDonnell, pride of the Delaware Blue Diamonds, had headhunting on her mind as she pushed into the Charleston bar. There sat Smokey O, the Blue Diamonds' pesky first base player, whose head Mac was hunting.

It was difficult to say whose ego was spoiling faster. Mac was in a slump, and Smokey O was on the bench.

Mac taunted Smokey O: "O'Neill is on the bench because that's where Coach Lefevre figures she can contribute the most."

Smokey O retaliated: "I'll tell you what, Mac. You may have something there, because I've had as many RBIs on the bench in the last two games as you've had at the plate."

Of such stuff is a championship club supposed to be made.

From there, it got worse.

Clarabelle's premise was that a team with Mac and me on it was a team that would go down in infamy.

She called me an agitator. She compared me to Billy Martin, the old New York Yankees manager. She said I was an irritant who could goad a club into performing when I arrived — except that my act was treacherous and that over time, it grated.

She said it was why Boston got rid of me. She said it was why Boston was in first place. "Smokey O may make her biggest contribution to a baseball club by getting traded. Boston learned it. Delaware may have to," she wrote.

118

Clarabelle humiliated Mac. She said Mac was a ballplayer with a past but no future, overstaying her welcome by riding on the reputation of an Olympic home run hit more than a decade ago. "There ought to be an organization called Baseball Anonymous, like Alcoholics Anonymous, for players like Mac who need help knowing when to quit," she wrote.

To weave her story of disruption and dissent, Clarabelle twisted the things I had said to her. In an admiring, if somewhat grudging, assessment of Mac, I had remarked, "Mac can carry the team, if she's on." Clarabelle turned it into a bitter and sarcastic assault that read: "Mac can carry the team — *if* she's on."

Clarabelle had asked me how Mac prepared for games, and I had answered truthfully, "She doesn't mix much. She keeps to herself." Clarabelle turned it into an indictment, making it sound as though I had critized Mac as a loner indifferent to the club's well-being.

Clarabelle had done her homework. She discovered and recounted all manner of stormy incidents between Mac and me, from the time Mac had knocked me down while I was still with Boston and I called her a "freakin' coward," to our prickly insults in the Charleston bar.

Clarabelle had gone to Boston, too. A lot of players who I thought were my friends said Delaware had made a fatal mistake by trading for me. At least, that's what Clarabelle had them saying.

Clarabelle concluded:

The betting here is that Boston wins the Eastern

119

Division. Boston doesn't have Smokey O anymore, and Mac doesn't have what it takes anymore.

It was a news story from hell. I read it twice. Then I panicked.

My phone rang, and I wouldn't answer it. At best, it would be a teammate full of hurt and questions. At worst, it would be a sportswriter feeding on the carrion.

It could even be Mac.

I drove to the ballpark. Coach Lefevre was in her office, as I knew she would be. There was a *Sports Illustrated* on her desk.

I threw myself on her mercy. "Coach, I said those things, but I didn't say them the way Clarabelle said that I did. You've got to believe me."

Lefevre's phone rang. Instead of answering it, she buzzed the switchboard through the intercom. "Hold my calls," she said, "unless it's a player."

She looked at me thoughtfully, then opened a desk drawer. She sorted through it until she found the check for five hundred dollars that she had made me write so I would stop baiting Mac in the newspapers.

"I believe you," Lefevre said, and she ripped up the check.

I sank onto her couch and leaned my head in my hands. "What am I going to do, Coach?"

The phone rang. "Hello," Lefevre said. "Hello, S.B. . . . It's all right, she's here. . . . Yes, in my office. . . . I know, I've had calls from sportswriters all morning. . . . Good idea, I can use you. I'll talk to you when you get here."

Lefevre hung up and said, "That was S.B., who is

a good friend to you. She was concerned because she couldn't reach you. She's going to come in to help field the questions from the press."

Somehow, the thought of S.B. taking the heat for me only made me feel worse. "Coach, I never meant to do anything that would hurt the club. I love playing here."

I was damn near choked up, and Lefevre just chuckled. "Smokey, you sound as though *you* believe Clarabelle's story. I've had my hands full dealing with the things you *have* done wrong. Don't you go confessing to things you haven't done. Let's talk a minute."

Lefevre had a coffee pot in her office. She poured each of us a cup and sat beside me on the couch.

"I've had my eye on you since your rookie year, when Shakespeare hit a hot smash at you in Boston, and you fielded it as caressingly as you'd pick up a newborn chick. You play this game with love, Smokey, and that's rare. That's real rare. Then there's the other side of you. You're a born troublemaker. You never met a rule you liked or a wisecrack you didn't. It kept you an outsider in Boston, because they didn't know what to do about you. You hung around more with the sportswriters than your teammates, and that's not good. I traded for both sides of you. I wanted a good ballplayer who could keep my clubhouse stirred up. I wanted someone who would push the limits and keep the other players loose. I figured I could handle you, although God knows it hasn't been easy. I've disciplined you more than I've disciplined any other player, and I've coached everything from Little League to pro ball."

She took a sip of coffee and continued. "For the most part, you've worked out the way I wanted. You shored up my infield and gave me a good leadoff hitter. By watching you around the veterans, Stryker got up her confidence. She's turned into the best damned relief pitcher in women's baseball. S.B.'s guardianship of you has brought out the best in her on the diamond and in the clubhouse. And the veterans won't let themselves slack off with you around. But I haven't been able to wean you from your wisecracks to the press, have I?"

"Oh God, Coach, I'm sorry. I should have listened to you."

"Some players spend hours before a game combing their hair just so. You spent your time polishing your quotes."

I winced.

"Go get yourself cleaned up, Smokey O. When S.B. comes in, we'll discuss what we want to say about this story. This is one time it won't hurt to polish a few quotes."

I had forgotten I was still in my running clothes. It had been a long morning.

"Coach, are you going to talk to Mac?"

"No, Smokey. That's for you to do."

And that's what I was *really* afraid of.

I didn't have many clothes on when S.B. came into the locker room. She gave me a pretty frank once-over and said, "You don't *seem* to have horns and a tail, but maybe Clarabelle got a better look than I did."

"S.B., are you mad at me?"

"Mad? No, not mad. Just — I don't know — resigned, I guess. Some of us worked kind of hard to try to keep this from happening."

"I know. I feel awful. It's my fault."

"It's not just your fault. Mac did her share. And we've got a snitch or two on this team, who gave Clarabelle all that inside information — although I suspect she got a lot of it from Mac."

"God, S.B., people all across the country are going to read that story and think it's true. Today of all days. It's the start of the biggest series of the year, and everybody's going to be talking about Clarabelle's story."

"Which is just what Clarabelle intended, I'm sure. Have you talked to Coach Lefevre yet?"

"Yes. She was pretty nice to me, but I still feel like I've been taken to the woodshed."

"If you're ready, let's go back to her office. Shakespeare and Zion are here, too, to help bail you out."

When we walked into Lefevre's office, Shakespeare caught me in a half nelson that wasn't meant to be gentle. "We could all clobber you," she said, "but we're going to save your ass, instead." She let me go.

Lefevre fanned out a stack of pink telephone messages. "These are the media calls already, and that's just from the ones who don't sleep late. We've got more sportswriters in town than usual, because of the interest in tonight's game, and they're all smelling blood in the water and moving in."

"Can I say something?" I said. "Listen, I feel like a jerk. I'm sorry, and I appreciate what you all are doing. I don't deserve it."

"Damn right you don't," Zion said. Since she was sitting near enough to me to kick my leg, she did. Then she relented. "Aw, Smokey, it's all right. You may be a jackass, but you're our jackass."

"Here's what we're going to do," Lefevre said. "We have to bury this story under an avalanche of counter-publicity. We have to be more credible than Clarabelle. We have to get the sportswriters on our side and make them want to go after Clarabelle, instead of us. The front-office staff is setting up the press conference room for you. Go out there and talk one-on-one with every reporter who comes in. No joint appearances — we want them to think they're getting exclusive interviews. They're more likely to report what you say if they think no one else has it. We're going to encourage the reporters to get here as soon as they can. I want our side of the story to be out by the time the radio and television stations do their noontime news. I want the fans to hear it from us before they have a chance to buy *Sports Illustrated* on their way home from work. If we don't win them over before they get to the ballpark tonight, they'll kill us."

S.B. nodded in agreement.

"While you four are out there doing interviews, I'll stay in my office and take the telephone calls from the national press." Lefevre went on, "Here's what we're going to say. Don't complain about the story. Don't attack Clarabelle. Say that she got her facts right, but she drew the wrong conclusion. Tell them there's more to this club than a couple of well-publicized spats that are nothing but old news, anyway."

"I know what," Zion said. "I can talk about how Smokey and Mac volunteered to do a clinic for city kids yesterday. I can say that's what this team is really like."

"That's great. That's exactly what we want," Lefevre said. "Be positive. Tell them we're going to disprove Clarabelle's interpretation by winning the division title." She turned to me. "As for you, Smokey, you get out there and eat crow. You tell those sportswriters it's your fault that Clarabelle got the wrong impression of you. You tell them that you've never been more thrilled in your life than to play on the same team as Mac MacDonnell. When I get the newspapers tomorrow, I better read that you're the sorriest ball player that ever gave a quote to a sportswriter. You got it?"

"Yes, Coach." I knew as well as Lefevre did that the sportswriters couldn't resist the spectacle of public contrition. It would put the story to rest.

The cost would be that my ego would take one hell of a pounding. But Lefevre knew that, too. As she sent us out to meet the press, she caught my eye and smiled.

CHAPTER FIFTEEN

The conversations in the locker room before game time were tense and resentful. The angry words that I overheard were directed at Clarabelle, but I was treated to a hefty dose of dirty looks.

As the players came in, S.B., Shakespeare and Zion kept up the missionary work that they had started with the sportswriters, defusing and deflecting the Blue Diamonds' outrage. Only this time, in the sanctuary of the clubhouse, they were outspoken and profane about what they thought of Clarabelle.

"*Someone* told her that crap," I heard Cranny say to Shakespeare.

"She made it *up*. Don't you understand? She fuckin' *made it* up," Shakespeare snapped.

They were arguing. I had never heard them argue before, and it was a frightening thing.

Mac came in, and it was as if she and I were the only two beings in the universe. Amid the chaos of inflamed players, discarded clothes, baseball gloves, cosmetics, uniforms and bats, Mac never looked at anything but me.

The voices around us ceased, like an orchestra that had lost its conductor, and Mac said, "Come here."

She jerked her head toward the showers. I followed.

In the privacy and stark sterility there, Mac said, "Tonight, after the game, come back to the ballpark. The players' entrance will be unlocked. Quarter 'til midnight. We're going to settle this between us, once and for all."

I was despairing and intimidated but unresisting, like the condemned who sees the gallows and hears the priest reading the Scripture. I owed this to Mac.

We returned to the locker room. Lefevre was waiting, but all she did was address the team. "We've got a very important game to play, so let's get focused. I'll be disappointed if you let yourselves get beat because of a magazine writer," she said.

We headed for the field, S.B. sticking with me every step of the way. We didn't talk.

There was a smattering of boos as we emerged from the dugout for our warmup, but mostly we heard cheers and applause. Lefevre had been right to have us get our side of the story out.

Boston was lying in wait for us. The Colonials were seated in the visitors' dugout, right legs crossed over left knees. All of them were reading *Sports Illustrated.*

If it hadn't been so infuriating, it would have been riotously funny. The sports photographers were shoving each other to get the best angle for a picture.

Mac stood by our dugout and signed autographs for a horde of fans that looked at her as though she was Joan of Arc. If she fell, they would mourn for her, because she had done so much for them. She was not the villain of this piece.

I scanned the press box. Clarabelle was not there.

This was as big a game as there could be. If the Blue Diamonds won, we would be tied with Boston for first place. If we lost, the Colonials would be two games out in front, and the sportswriters could start working on our obituary.

The Chief and Lorraine of Terror, the two best pitchers in the Women's Baseball League, were starting. Both of them were money pitchers with a lot of pride.

As if either of them needed more of an edge, it was a pitcher's night, hot and muggy. While the steam heat kept them as loose and grooved as a long distance runner, the baseball bats would feel just a tick heavier on the hitters' shoulders. While the pitchers found their rhythm, the hitters would have to will themselves to concentrate in the sweaty humidity, and likely as not, a mosquito would settle on a hitter's neck just as she was ready to swing.

As the Chief and Lorraine of Terror warmed up in the bullpens, the front office outdid itself with hoopla for the big game. Bands paraded across the diamond and local celebrities said a few words to the crowd. The national anthem was sung by a huge combined choir from several local high schools, which sounded fine but was as slow as a garden slug getting off the field. Even though the choir members hadn't done anything more strenuous than sing, they were streaming sweat as they exited.

I didn't think they'd ever get out of the way for the game to start, and I was desperate for the sense of normality and familiarity that playing baseball would bring.

Finally! "Batter up," the umpire said, and the Colonials sent Addie Gomez to the plate to face the Chief.

The Chief was looking nonchalant and pitching sharp. Addie took a fastball for a strike, fouled a curve ball away, laid off an inside pitch for a ball and then hit a routine grounder toward S.B. at second.

S.B. fielded the ball cleanly and threw sure and true to me.

And I dropped it.

I hadn't made an error like that since Little League. I was stunned. So were the fans, who even forgot to boo.

Clarabelle was doing this to me.

Addie grinned like a goblin. "Hey, don't choke or nothing, Smokey," she said.

Rheta Wood, who could hit, was next up, and she sent Addie all the way to third base on a nifty hit-and-run single. Addie scored on a sacrifice fly before the Chief shut Boston down. We trailed, 1–0.

I was remorseful and apologized to the Chief, but she waved me off. I couldn't figure out whether she was telling me to forget about it or to get the hell away. I got the hell away.

The fans were clapping rhythmically, beseeching us to get the run back, when I scuffed at the white lines of the batter's box and glanced at Lorraine of Terror. She faced home plate with shoulders squared and a conquering look on her face.

She struck me out.

The fans were ungodly silent, and I wished for their boos and their contempt. Their muteness was too much like a death watch. Maybe they were coming to believe what Clarabelle had written.

S.B. struck out, and Mac did, too. The run that I let in loomed very, very large.

The pitchers went at it. If Lorraine of Terror could strike out the side, so could the Chief. Boston barely managed a foul ball in the top of the second, and we had a real pitching duel going. The pitchers lived on strikeouts and groundouts, and the hitters died on them.

When the Chief stalked off the mound after pitching the top of the ninth, the Blue Diamonds were still behind by that crummy, unearned run that I had given away. We were down to our last three outs — and maybe down to our last chance to overtake Boston for the season.

The fans were jittery, and their anxious voices

came to us like the nervous whinny of a horse. The bottom of our batting order was due up: Chang, Gonzales and a pinch hitter for the Chief. Stryker started warming up in the bullpen.

Lorraine of Terror was still as commanding as she had been in the first inning. Marcia Chang, desperate to find an edge, did the only thing she could think of. When Lorraine of Terror threw one inside, Marcia leaned into it. It scalded her on her upper arm, but we had ourselves a runner.

This was no time for macho hitting. Gonzales dropped a beauty of a bunt toward first base. Marcia lit out for second, and Gonzales scooted into first just a flash before Lorraine of Terror got there to cover.

We had runners at first and second, nobody out, and the fans were on their feet and screaming.

Lefevre sent in Mulligan to hit for the Chief. With two strikes on her, she swung mightily and smashed a fly ball to the warning track in straightaway center field. Chang and Gonzales tagged up and advanced a base.

The Blue Diamonds had two runners in scoring position, with one out. We were one base away from tying this game, two away from winning it, and it was my turn to bat.

All a ballplayer can ask for is a chance to redeem herself. This was mine, and I wanted it badly. I wanted to atone for my error in the first, I wanted to face Mac that night cleansed by victory, and I wanted to ram *Sports Illustrated* down Clarabelle's throat.

I fouled off the first pitch from Lorraine of

Terror, took two high pitches for balls, fouled off two more and took another ball for a full count. Then the real war of attrition began.

Lorraine of Terror was damned if she was going to let me beat her. She threw tantalizing pitches that were too close to the strike zone to take, so I kept hacking and fouling them off and praying for one that I could handle.

I lost track of how many there were, but Gonzales told me later that I fouled off eight in a row. The fans moaned in torment every time.

Then Lorraine of Terror slyly threw a change-up. I barely ticked it with my bat, not enough to deflect it, and it plopped into the catcher's mitt and stayed there. Strike three, and I was gone — no atonement, no victory, no revenge, just the second out in the bottom of the ninth.

I headed morosely for the far corner of the dugout, but Lefevre called me to sit beside her. She put her arm around my shoulders. "Be proud, Smokey O. That's the toughest out I've ever seen."

"It's still an out, Coach," I said, inconsolable. Lefevre left her arm around me, and the cameras started clicking, prying cold-bloodedly into my desolation.

S.B. was at the plate, and the Boston Colonials did the unthinkable. With first base open, they elected to walk her intentionally — and pitch to Mac.

It was a cruel psych job. The fans erupted in insulted outrage, throwing popcorn, peanuts, empty cups and other debris onto the field. Zion and Shakespeare screamed obscenities at Boston until the first base umpire told them to shut up or he'd run them out of the game.

I wondered who thought of it. Coach Pettibone didn't have that much imagination.

With copies of *Sports Illustrated* still strewn throughout the visitors' dugout, Mac went to bat.

Boston wasn't done hexing her yet. The Colonials brought in their center fielder to be a fifth infielder. Anything Mac hit on the ground would need eyes to skitter past that wall of defenders.

Bases loaded, two out, the bottom of the ninth. Mac against Lorraine of Terror. The season had come down to this.

This was the way it should be. This was the way it had to be. We would live or die with Mac.

I knew what I had to do. I wanted Mac to win this game for us, even more than I had wanted to win it myself. I didn't care what she did to me at the midnight hour that night.

"Mac!" I shouted, as I scrambled from the bench. "Come on!"

I flipped the bill of my hat around, making it a rally cap, and I strained forward against the railing that separated the dugout from the field, willing her to get a hit.

"Come on!"

The Blue Diamonds were with me. They put on their rally caps and stood at the railing and they shouted.

Mac looked at us. She surveyed the five infielders. She stared levelly at Lorraine of Terror. She looked long at me.

Then she stepped in. The first pitch, shearing through the muggy night air, was a called strike; the second a ball. The next one Mac scorched foul down the third base line. Another ball evened the count at two balls and two strikes, and then Mac connected solidly and unspectacularly with an outside pitch.

Not Clarabelle's national ridicule, not five infielders, not Lucifer himself could have stopped that hit, which just skimmed over the reach of Rheta Wood's timed leap and rolled into the vast expanse of an empty center field.

Marcia Chang scored, Gonzales scored, and the Blue Diamonds won the game, 2–1. In the indescribable bedlam at home plate, Mac fought through the crush to find me. She gripped my arms. Her eyes were those of a sinner who has been forgiven, and she said, "Tonight."

CHAPTER SIXTEEN

By the midnight light I returned to Du Pont Stadium, and I prayed for the players' entrance to be locked. It wasn't.

The high stadium walls stood like a monument above me as I pushed my way into the ballpark's innards and walked, as silent as a trespasser, through the shadowy corridors lit by the pale glow of the security bulbs.

I knew this ballpark; I knew it the way you know your grandmother's house. It is not yours, but you love it and you draw solace from knowing how many steps it will take you to come to the clubhouse and how the bats inside will be stacked just so, the same way you know that the ancient doily will be under the majolica bowl on your grandmother's dining room table.

This night was different. This night there was no comfort. The drafts and the dark reaches where light never shone made the ballpark feel like a sepulcher, and I was a disturbance that did not belong.

Mac was not in the locker room, and so I walked past Lefevre's office and S.B.'s meticulously neat cubicle and the extra-large pink sweatshirt that Cranny had left behind, and I made my way toward the field.

As I came through the dugout, the sultry night air carried the sound of the carillon at the University of Delaware striking the quarter hour — one ghostly chime that shimmered and faded.

Mac was standing at home plate. Her right hand was propped on a bat that looked ash-blond and slick in the reflected light. She was dressed in white slacks and a white sports shirt, open at the throat. She looked like a relic from Victorian tennis.

Well, the good guys always wear white, I told myself. I had on a pair of washed-out jeans and a dark blue T-shirt, half ruffian and half cat burglar.

"Behold, the cover girl cometh," Mac said mockingly.

I never broke stride or looked up until I stopped at home plate across from her. Surprisingly, she didn't look angry.

"I have been on the cover of *Sports Illustrated* before," Mac said, "but never with quite so much fuss."

"I know about those other covers. I put them up in my room at home. It was one of the things that made me want to play baseball."

"So where are those covers now?"

"On the scrap heap — the same as the player."

Before I could even flinch, Mac had me by the scruff of the neck. She had amazing reflexes, collaring me just as easily as she snared fly balls. No wonder she could hit Lorraine of Terror when I couldn't.

"It was a joke, Mac, honest to God," I said. Those fading magazine covers were still on the wall in my room at my mother's house.

I thought about what Coach Lefevre had said to me earlier, that I never met a wisecrack I didn't like. It was true. It was still true. Even when the jig was up, I couldn't stop myself.

"You make it very difficult," Mac said.

"To do what?"

"To —"

We heard the jangle of keys and a thud. Mac looked stricken. She let me go and sprinted to the dugout and down the corridor toward the clubhouse. Not knowing what else to do, I followed.

Miss Jewel lay crumpled in the dim concrete passageway, her keys and a pile of laundry, topped by Cranny's pink sweatshirt, fallen beside her. She was sneaking around at this late hour to do her work, as though she could hide from her own health in the dark of night.

Mac knelt beside Miss Jewel and gently rolled her onto her back. She tipped Miss Jewel's head back and listened for her breath. She blew into Miss Jewel's mouth and felt her neck for a pulse.

"Christ! No breath and no pulse! Get to a phone and call an ambulance," Mac said. "I'll do CPR."

There were pay phones on the levels above us, but it would take me time to get there, and I might be blocked by locked doors. The phones down here were all in locked offices.

I grabbed the bat that Mac had with her and ran for the clubhouse. At Lefevre's office I swung the bat and shattered the large glass window that gave the coach a commanding view of the locker room, then reached through and unlocked the door.

I phoned 911 and told the dispatcher about Miss Jewel, remembering to tell him to send the paramedics to the players' entrance. As I hung up, the emergency siren already was wailing.

I ran back to help Mac with the cardiopulmonary resuscitation, deeply thankful that the officials of the Women's Baseball League made all the players take an emergency CPR course as part of spring training.

Mac looked drained. CPR was hard work and emotionally grueling. "I can spell you," I said and knelt beside Miss Jewel.

Mac pulled away long enough to take a few deep breaths herself, then came back to help, and together we did the mouth-to-mouth breathing and the chest compressions, moving to the life-giving rhythm — "one-and, two-and, three-and" — willing Miss Jewel to live.

At one point her breath and pulse fluttered, feathery soft, but they flickered away before we could rejoice, and we fought fiercely for her life again. *One-and, two-and, three-and . . .*

The screaming sound of the siren drew nearer,

until it cut off abruptly as the emergency van braked and we heard the paramedics approaching us, the wheels of a gurney clattering on the concrete floor.

The paramedics came forward purposefully in their starched white uniforms, as welcome as angels. We made way and they moved in.

They worked quickly to stabilize Miss Jewel and get her to the life-saving equipment in their van, but even in their precise professionalism, they stole a fraction of a second to glance at us.

They had to be thinking that it was not every night that you get summoned to a scene by Mac MacDonnell and Smokey O. And what the hell were we doing together and doing at the ballpark so late at night?

I wish I knew.

The paramedics invited us along as they took Miss Jewel to the emergency center on Main Street. We sat crammed together on a bench in the back, riding in tense silence, as the van rushed through the deserted Newark streets, its emergency flashers reflected crazily in rows of dark windows in silent houses and the University of Delaware's quiet halls.

At the emergency center Mac told the desk attendant as much as we knew, and then we sat in the waiting room, staring at a television showing a late-night movie without taking any of it in.

We broke our silence only once, when Mac asked me, "How did you get to a phone so fast?"

"I used the one in Lefevre's office. I took your bat and smashed her window and broke in."

"Oh. Good thinking."

After a while, a physician came to us with an expression that was indecipherable and a stride that was tired but not sorrowful.

We stood.

"Thanks to the two of you, her prognosis is good," the physician said.

Mac and I looked at each other with unspeakable gratitude.

"I better call Lefevre," Mac said.

"Tell her I'm sorry about her window," I said.

"Good morning," the broadcast began on the *Today* show. "Two players from the Delaware Blue Diamonds saved the life of their clubhouse manager last night in a dramatic rescue using CPR. We'll be joining Mac MacDonnell and Smokey O'Neill live at a news conference at Du Pont Stadium in about an hour."

Everything had happened very fast. By the time Lefevre arrived to collect us, the director of the emergency room had been notified, and he came in, despite the ungodly hour. He turned out to be a little on the publicity-hungry side, and Lefevre figured that she had better take control before he did.

She drew us aside. "I'm going to have to call the newspaper and tell them what happened," she said. She looked at Mac. "And there's going to have to be a press conference, first thing in the morning."

Mac nodded. "I'll do it," she said.

I was startled. Mac had hardly granted an interview since the Olympics, and here she was agreeing to a press conference that had all the makings of a media gang bang. I decided not to try to figure it out. This whole night had me feeling like Alice on the wrong side of the looking glass.

Lefevre telephoned the Wilmington *News Journal*'s sports desk just before the deadline for the Sports Final edition. The editors did what they could, remaking the front page to include a box briefly reporting what Mac and I had done and announcing the press conference.

It made for a chaotic newspaper. You had all the stuff about Mac and me and *Sports Illustrated,* plus the game against Boston, plus Miss Jewel. I don't know how the readers sorted it out. I barely could.

Lefevre really was magnificent that night. You'd never know that she had been awakened to handle a crisis after one of the most emotional games she had ever coached. She got the front office arranging the press conference, she called Miss Jewel's family herself, and she dealt with the emergency room staff, all without offending anyone.

When she was sure everything was squared away, she guided Mac and me to her car and drove to an all-night diner. I thought I didn't want anything, but I was famished, and so was Mac.

No one talked for a while. Lefevre sipped coffee while Mac and I ate. Then Lefevre casually asked us what had happened. We barely answered at first, but soon the words came rushing out of us and we told her every detail of every terrifying moment.

"She wasn't breathing," Mac said. "She didn't have a pulse. I've never been so frightened in my life."

"You were frightened?" I said. "You seemed calm

to me. Dead calm, like you were getting ready for batting practice, or something."

"Hell, no. I was scared to death. But I didn't want to panic you. Shit, I didn't want to panic *me*."

"Well, it worked. I figured I had to be as cool as you. I just took a second until I thought about the quickest way to get to a phone."

"You could have used a key," Lefevre said drily. "As I understand this story, Miss Jewel's keys were lying there beside her."

Lefevre was right. I could have used the key, but I never thought about it at the time. I just grabbed the bat and ran.

"Ooops," I said, and we laughed, laughing harder and harder until the tears came to our eyes and we cried, crying for Miss Jewel and for relief and for the tragedy that could have been.

The late-night waitresses stood away from us in a cluster under the garish fluorescent light and made comments out of the sides of their mouths, looking at us as though we were all candidates for the drunk tank. But we didn't care.

Eventually we wound down. Lefevre paid the bill and drove us back to the stadium, where our cars were. Dawn overtook us as we stood in the parking lot, not wanting to go. It was peaceful here, and the birds were singing their hymns to the morning, and the ballpark was as cool as a cathedral with the awful power to outwit death itself.

I shivered, overcome by fatigue and emotion. Lefevre noticed. She cupped my chin in her hand and raised it until I had no choice but to look at her.

"Are you all right?" she asked.

"Yes."

"You're sure?"

"Yes."

"Then perhaps you'd like to tell me what you were doing at the ballpark at midnight?"

I stiffened as though someone had stuck a gun against my back. I had no idea what to say. Dreadful seconds ticked away while I tried to decide whether I was more afraid of Lefevre or Mac.

It was becoming quite clear that Lefevre wasn't about to release me when Mac spoke. "She doesn't know. I'm the only one who knows, and whatever it was, it didn't happen."

Lefevre let me go. She switched her attention to Mac, who was regarding both of us with a teasing smile. No wonder — she had a secret she was keeping, and she'd just left me dangling at Lefevre's mercy until she felt like bailing me out.

"You'll be asked at the press conference," Lefevre said.

"I'll handle it. Trust me."

Lefevre looked at the player who had brought her an Olympic gold medal, who had brought her three W.B.L. Crowns, who had brought her a must-win game the night before. "I always have," Lefevre said. "I'll see both of you back here in about an hour."

I went home, showered and changed my clothes. I was getting my second wind, the andrenaline pumping as I thought about the press conference. It was going to be a madhouse. It would have been bad enough just because of the events — Miss Jewel, the competition with Boston, the *Sports Illustrated* story — but with Mac there, the sportswriters were *really* going to salivate.

* * * * *

The press conference room was packed. The front office had brought in huge urns of coffee, a plastic cooler of ice water, dozens of doughnuts and a punch bowl full of raspberry yogurt. Like animals at a zoo, the press corps was a little less surly on a full stomach.

Every seat was taken, and more sportswriters were slouching against the walls. There were people that I had never seen before, and I guessed that the editors had sent in some of their news reporters, too.

The bright bank of lights from the television cameras gave the room all the friendliness of a police interrogation chamber. I wondered what we were in for.

The director of the emergency room, the owner of the Blue Diamonds and even the governor were there to read statements. It's amazing who will show up to claim credit when somebody's life has been saved. The reporters listened without bothering to conceal their boredom. The director, the owner and the governor wouldn't even get a mention in the stories; their hope for publicity was the cable networks that were broadcasting this media circus live.

I was shaking when we finally sat down at the table, microphones pointing at us like so many rifles in a firing squad. I shouldn't have worried. I was an old story. It was Mac they wanted.

Mac was cool. She recounted the rescue of Miss Jewel, repeating her responses patiently for the inevitable crew of reporters who were too stupid to get it on the first telling.

But that wasn't the story the press had come for. They would report it, all right, because lifesaving was good copy, but what they were lusting for was the gossip.

"So, Mac, what did you think of the *Sports Illustrated* story?"

"I didn't give it much thought."

"Come on. Did you think it was accurate?"

"In a manner of speaking. If I'd asked a chicken to write a history of foxes, I think the result would have been about the same."

The sportswriters laughed — a bad sign. It meant they were picturing vicious stories in their diabolical heads.

"Hey, Mac, I thought I remembered that you and Clarabelle were friends."

"You must have a better memory than I do."

"What did you think about Clarabelle writing that you're a ballplayer with a past but no future?"

Mac looked deadly. "I wish I had your nerve, to ask a question like that. Why don't you ask the Boston Colonials if they think I've lost it?"

"Mac, what about Smokey O? Clarabelle got that right, didn't she, that you two don't get along?"

"Not true," Mac said evenly.

"Smokey? What do you say about that?"

"The same as Mac," I said cheerfully. It was news to me, too, but what the hell. The reporters looked irritated. They hate it when they can't get a fight going.

"Say, what were you two doing at the ballpark so late last night?"

Mac shrugged. "Catching the Goldrushers' game from the West Coast on the satellite dish," she said.

145

It sounded plausible to me, but the reporters looked skeptical. One of them, sitting in the center of the room, shook her head and got up to get a refill on coffee. As if on cue, the door in the back opened, and Clarabelle let herself in. She walked calmly to the vacated seat, as though it had been left for her.

A little circle cleared around her as the other reporters shifted away. Clarabelle's entrance couldn't have been more startling if she'd come in like Lady Godiva on her horse. Utter silence prevailed. Some television cameras left us and trained on her.

Clarabelle had the nerves of an assassin. I'll say that for her. She sat there as though she hadn't been after us with her poison pen, as though her appearance at the press conference was as natural as flowers at a tea party.

Although the reporters had been calling out to us, Clarabelle raised her hand and said sweetly, "May I ask a question?"

In a low voice, too soft for the microphones to pick up, Mac said, "Smokey." With a flick of her gaze, she directed my attention to the large cooler of ice water.

I understood. "I'm with you," I whispered.

Like outlaws on the lam, we bounded to the water cooler. Mac knocked off the top, and we hefted it, heavy as it was, then bulled through the crowd as reporters scattered, and in one glorious heave, upended it over Clarabelle's pretty head.

She shrieked as the ice and water cascaded over her, sopping her and turning her pastel designer blouse and slacks transparent and making them cling to every curve, angle and nipple of her well-made body. The television cameras recorded each reckless moment of it for the sports highlights films, which would ensure forever that Clarabelle would be remembered, not for her prose, but for one of the greatest public humiliations of all time.

We fell away, laughing. Forgive us, for we knew what we did.

The other reporters did a very unreporter-like thing. They applauded.

The press conference was over. Mac and I beat it out of there, got in our cars and drove away, not wanting to talk to anybody, least of all Lefevre.

I desperately wanted some sleep. I was nearly home when a new thought hit me. When Mac wanted me to help her dump the water cooler on Clarabelle, she called me "Smokey," not "O'Neill." It was the first time. I thought about it, and I almost didn't get to sleep.

CHAPTER SEVENTEEN

Coach Lefevre sat both Mac and me down for the second game against the Boston Colonials. She said we had been through enough.

Not that the club needed us. Our escapades had taken the pressure off, and the Blue Diamonds merrily rolled along to a 9–2 victory that gave the team sole possession of first place.

Mac and I sat together in the dugout and talked baseball throughout the game. I was a little starstruck by her attention. Never mind how long I had played on the team, I was in awe of Mac all over again. (S.B. knew it, I could tell. She gave me a smile and a wink and left me to handle it by myself.)

It hardly seemed possible that only a day ago, *Sports Illustrated* had gone on sale and we had faced Boston in a game as tense as a high-wire act with no net. It seemed even less possible that we had been called upon to save Miss Jewel and catapulted into national attention.

The best part was paying Clarabelle back. The clubhouse was already decorated with a huge blowup of a photo showing Mac and me dousing Clarabelle. The water cooler itself had been purloined from the front office and set in front of Mac's locker with the inscription: "Blue Diamonds 1, Press 0."

After the game, Mac walked out with me. "Come on, Smokey, let's go for a ride," she said.

I couldn't stand it anymore. "Why are you calling me that?"

"What? Smokey? It's your name, isn't it?"

"Yes, but —"

"Then shut up."

I shut up. We went to her car. It was a sports car, and she drove it well.

"Where are we going?" I asked.

"My place. To finish what we started."

"Mac —"

"Chill out, Smokey. Just once, do what you're told."

I subsided. Mac turned on the radio. The station was playing "Crystal in Time," that heart-stopping song by the NaySayers:

"This night should never have to end.

Let's savor one last glass of wine,
And if we never meet again,
At least we had this crystal in time."

I had a feeling of suspended animation. With the song playing and the car beating down the road through the warm summer night, I didn't care if we ever got anywhere. I wanted to stay here forever, like a ghost in time, while the past still felt good and the future couldn't get to me.

Mac drove on, urging the sports car through the hills and turns of back roads to get to her house. She owned a five-acre property about ten miles outside of Newark. It was too dark to see much, but I'd been told that her lot was mostly wooded, with a tennis court and a swimming pool that could be glassed in during the winter.

I was nervous, but I felt better when Mac took me into her kitchen and invited me to sit at the table. There is something utterly unintimidating about being in someone's kitchen, even one as nice as this one, with its custom-made cabinets and state-of-the-art appliances from the microwave to the espresso machine. Someone still had to do the dishes here.

Mac left the lights low and got us a couple of beers from her refrigerator.

"To the Blue Diamonds," she said, and we drank. Then she said, looking right at me, "I brought you here because I wanted to thank you for the year I've had."

I shoved myself away from the table as though she'd tossed a snake onto it. "Goddamn it, Mac, don't make fun of me."

"I'm not, you stupid jerk. Sit down and listen."

"Did Lefevre tell you to do this?"

"Damn it, no. Now sit down."

I sat.

"I was furious when Lefevre traded for you. She called me in and told me about it as soon as it was done. I knew before you did. I said to Lefevre, 'How can you do this to me?' And she said, 'You think I did this because of you?' I said yes, and she said, 'Then maybe you better think about why I would.' I slammed out of there, as mad as I've ever been. I couldn't believe it. You make that God-awful crack to the sportswriters, and Lefevre trades for you. I couldn't have felt worse if she'd walked out to center field in front of a stadium full of fans and slapped me."

Mac took a deep breath. "It's no secret I was struggling, no secret I was having doubts, wondering if I was hurting the club more than helping. Then you arrive, you little shit, and I hit a home run and go four for four, and it's the first game I feel focused, feel the fires burning, in a long, long time. So I did what Lefevre said I should do. I thought about it. I didn't like doing it, but I did."

I looked at her as she took a draw on her beer.

"You're a pain in the butt, Smokey O'Neill, you know that? You're exactly what Lefevre wanted you to be. And even though I knew that Lefevre was playing a head game with me, you were still a spur in my side, and I couldn't stop feeling that way, no matter how much I wanted to ignore you. And the next thing I knew, I was playing, really *playing*, like a kid in college who prayed that she'd impress a certain coach putting together an Olympic team. You won't believe this, but I started to like you pretty early on. Maybe it was the night we stayed late, and I hit all those balls at you, and you just stood there and took it. Certainly by the time I hit those four home runs and you had to carry my bags." Mac laughed. "But you were still a brat, and I figured you deserved to be treated like one. And if you could help my game by getting to me, I could help your game by riding the hell out of you. So I did."

"I guess it worked," I said. "I'm playing better and making more of a contribution than I ever thought I would at this stage of my career."

Mac shook her head. "But I let it get out of hand. I should have stopped it when Claire came around. I should have known what she would do."

"But we got her back, didn't we?"

"You bet we did. They'll write about it in her obituary, God damn her eyes."

We laughed. The more we thought about it, the funnier it got, until we were laughing so hard that we had to prop ourselves against the table.

"You know," Mac said, "no matter what I did to you, you just played harder. When I was going up to bat in the ninth yesterday, and you hollered at me with your rally cap on, I couldn't believe it, after all you'd been through. I looked at you, and I knew I was going to get a hit. But even before the game turned out the way it did, I wanted to talk to you last night and thank you for what you've done for me, and I wanted to put an end to all the grief between us."

She shook her head and smiled. "You're something else, Smokey O. That's a good name for a ballplayer, you know? I didn't dare call you that before, because I was afraid you'd hear in my voice what I really thought about you."

"Mac, whatever you want to do is fine with me. You're the best that ever played this game. You're the best."

I could scarcely believe what was happening as we sat together in Mac's kitchen. I was happy and relaxed and awestruck, as though I'd been cast under a spell by a benevolent enchanter.

"Mac?"

"What?"

"Do you remember the night we all went out to dinner in Charleston, and Shakespeare did those toasts?"

"And you got drunk out of your mind, and S.B. and I had to put you to bed? Yes, I remember."

"Did you — did you tip your wine glass at me that night?"

"Why would I do that?"

"I don't know. Did you?"

"It doesn't seem like something I would do. Not then."

"I know that. But did you?"

"It's a mystery, isn't it?"

"Did you?"

Mac laughed. "Smokey, I'm not going to lay all your worries to rest at one time. I've got to leave you something to think about."

The magic went out of the night just a little. I had wanted it to be true, had wanted to know it was true. "All right," I said. "I suppose you ought to drive me back before it gets much later."

"Stay a while, Smokey. I still owe you something."

Mac came over to me. She bunched my shirt below the collar in her hands, lifted me from my chair and pinned me against the wall. I looked at her warily.

"You don't know if I'm going to kiss you or hit you, do you?" she taunted lightly.

I said nothing. I didn't know.

"You don't even know what you want — or what you deserve, do you?"

She placed her right palm against my cheek, as if measuring me for a blow. Unresisting, I braced for it. I had meant what I said when I told her that anything she wanted to do was fine with me.

Then Mac slipped her hand to the back of my neck caressingly, and her lips met mine. She kissed me tenderly, then exploringly, then possessively.

Nothing I had ever done before had felt so right.

"You want to," she said, more statement than question.

"I've never wanted anything like I want this."

Mac led me upstairs to her room, passion burning in me like a fever. I was so turned on that I was only vaguely aware of the mementos and prizes around me — the darkly gleaming trophies, the photographs and even the American flag that Mac and Coach Lefevre had hoisted after the Olympic triumph so many years before.

"Take off your clothes," Mac said.

I couldn't look at her as I did so, but I knew she was watching me intently, watching the buttons and the zipper come undone to make my body ready for her. When I was naked, she put me face down on her bed and massaged my back, her hands commanding but kind. My muscles turned to water under her touch. She stroked my hair.

Mac turned me over. Her eyes considered me as she took off her own clothes then lowered herself onto the bed beside me.

"I've wanted you," she said. "I've wanted you from the moment you came into the clubhouse and stood there, cocky and daring, and I wanted to subdue the fighter in you."

"What took you so long?" I groaned.

Mac laid her body against mine, and I was out of control. I could not tell which was sweeter, touching her or being touched, nor could I tell the difference. Her desire was mine, and mine, hers.

She caressed my skin and rubbed against me, and her lips and tongue roamed over my body, lingering long on my breasts. Her hand parted my thighs, and she found me drenched and frenzied. She stroked and teased and stroked and teased and kissed. Then I was nothing but sensation and came and came and came again until I was emptied and the tears washed from my eyes.

Mac cradled me in her arms, brushed away my tears and held me until I was calm. I turned and kissed the soft curves of her neck. I pressed my lips against hers in a demand that she yield to me.

"Yes," Mac consented in a whisper of longing, and I was on her, not gentle, wanting to do things to her body that she would never forget.

My mouth teased her breasts. My nipples rubbed against her. My fingers probed into her, but not enough to give her the release she craved. I lay full length on top of her, and she writhed against me.

I kissed her smooth, taut belly, lower, ever lower, but not giving her what she wanted, until she couldn't take it anymore.

"Fuck you, Smokey O," she gasped. "Do it!"

I did.

She bucked and shuddered when she came and dug her fingers into my shoulders and cried out in wordless ardor.

We lay exhausted. Soon we were laughing with the joy and improbability of being together.

Mac raised up and pinned me against the bed. "I'm going to pay you back," she said congenially.

"I thought you might," I said.

She did worse to me than I had to her, tormenting me with slow lovemaking. Her hands were magic and mischief, and her mouth was more of the same. Her eyes were fire and salvation, and this time, as she aroused me, I was aware of her, as she wanted me to be, aware that I was with Mac MacDonnell, who was the best that could be, and when finally she brought me to climax, I called out her name.

The Delaware Blue Diamonds won the division. Then the club beat the Sacramento Goldrushers to win the Women's Baseball League Crown. Mac was named the Most Valuable Player for the season, and S.B. won MVP honors in the Crown championship series.

Mac retired after that year. She said it was one more year than she deserved, and she wasn't going to push her luck. Although she had a lot of offers, she left professional baseball. Instead, she coached at the University of Delaware and did free clinics for kids, and she came to the ballpark to sit in the stands and watch me play.

S.B. had a stellar career. She won the batting title five years in a row, set the record for double plays in a single season by a second base player, and set the all-time record for hits in a career. She was the Most Valuable Player three times. When Lefevre retired, S.B. was named player-coach, and after she quit playing, she stayed on as the coach. Like Lefevre before her, she had the right touch for guiding the Blue Diamonds.

Miss Jewel recovered and went back to work, retiring only when Lefevre did. Her daughter Melinda signed on to work for S.B. as the clubhouse manager.

I didn't have a bad career myself. I led the league in stolen bases twice, and I set the record for errorless games in a row by a first base player. But nothing ever compared with my first season with the Delaware Blue Diamonds.

I finished my playing under S.B., then went into the broadcast booth. Mac said snidely that I should have been there all along.

Many years later, after an old-timers' game when we were all feeling mellow and nostalgic, Mac finally told me whether she had, in truth, meant to tip her wine glass at me that rainy night in Charleston.

But that's our secret.

A few of the publications of
THE NAIAD PRESS, INC.
P.O. Box 10543 • Tallahassee, Florida 32302
Phone (904) 539-5965
Toll-Free Order Number: 1-800-533-1973
Mail orders welcome. Please include 15% postage.

SMOKEY O by Celia Cohen. 176 pp. Relationships on the playing
field.   ISBN 1-56280-057-4 $9.95

KATHLEEN O'DONALD by Penny Hayes. 256 pp. Rose and
Kathleen find each other and employment in 1909 NYC.
                                                ISBN 1-56280-070-1   9.95

STAYING HOME by Elisabeth Nonas. 256 pp. Molly and Alix
want a baby . . . or do they?   ISBN 1-56280-076-0   10.95

TRUE LOVE by Jennifer Fulton. 240 pp. Six lesbians searching for
love in all the "right" places.   ISBN 1-56280-035-3   9.95

GARDENIAS WHERE THERE ARE NONE by Molleen Zanger.
176 pp. Why is Melanie inextricably drawn to the old house?
                                                ISBN 1-56280-056-6   9.95

MICHAELA by Sarah Aldridge. 256 pp. A "Sarah Aldridge"
romance.   ISBN 1-56280-055-8   10.95

KEEPING SECRETS by Penny Mickelbury. 208 pp. A Gianna
Maglione Mystery. First in a series.   ISBN 1-56280-052-3   9.95

THE ROMANTIC NAIAD edited by Katherine V. Forrest &
Barbara Grier. 336 pp. Love stories by Naiad Press authors.
                                                ISBN 1-56280-054-X   14.95

UNDER MY SKIN by Jaye Maiman. 336 pp. A Robin Miller
mystery. 3rd in a series.   ISBN 1-56280-049-3.   10.95

STAY TOONED by Rhonda Dicksion. 144 pp. Cartoons — 1st
collection since *Lesbian Survival Manual.*   ISBN 1-56280-045-0   9.95

CAR POOL by Karin Kallmaker. 272pp. Lesbians on wheels
and then some!   ISBN 1-56280-048-5   9.95

NOT TELLING MOTHER: STORIES FROM A LIFE by Diane
Salvatore. 176 pp. Her 3rd novel.   ISBN 1-56280-044-2   9.95

GOBLIN MARKET by Lauren Wright Douglas. 240pp. A Caitlin
Reece Mystery. 5th in a series.   ISBN 1-56280-047-7   9.95

LONG GOODBYES by Nikki Baker. 256 pp. A Virginia Kelly
mystery. 3rd in a series.   ISBN 1-56280-042-6   9.95

INTRODUCING AMANDA VALENTINE by Rose Beecham.
256 pp. An Amanda Valentine Mystery. First in a series.
ISBN 1-56280-021-3   9.95

UNCERTAIN COMPANIONS by Robbi Sommers. 204 pp.
Steamy, erotic novel.   ISBN 1-56280-017-5   9.95

A TIGER'S HEART by Lauren W. Douglas. 240 pp. A Caitlin
Reece mystery. 4th in a series.   ISBN 1-56280-018-3   9.95

PAPERBACK ROMANCE by Karin Kallmaker. 256 pp. A
delicious romance.   ISBN 1-56280-019-1   9.95

MORTON RIVER VALLEY by Lee Lynch. 304 pp. Lee Lynch at
her best!   ISBN 1-56280-016-7   9.95

THE LAVENDER HOUSE MURDER by Nikki Baker. 224 pp. A
Virginia Kelly Mystery. 2nd in a series.   ISBN 1-56280-012-4   9.95

PASSION BAY by Jennifer Fulton. 224 pp. Passionate romance,
virgin beaches, tropical skies.   ISBN 1-56280-028-0   9.95

STICKS AND STONES by Jackie Calhoun. 208 pp. Contemporary
lesbian lives and loves.   ISBN 1-56280-020-5   9.95

DELIA IRONFOOT by Jeane Harris. 192 pp. Adventure for Delia
and Beth in the Utah mountains.   ISBN 1-56280-014-0   9.95

UNDER THE SOUTHERN CROSS by Claire McNab. 192 pp.
Romantic nights Down Under.   ISBN 1-56280-011-6   9.95

RIVERFINGER WOMEN by Elana Nachman/Dykewomon.
208 pp. Classic Lesbian/feminist novel.   ISBN 1-56280-013-2   8.95

A CERTAIN DISCONTENT by Cleve Boutell. 240 pp. A unique
coterie of women.   ISBN 1-56280-009-4   9.95

GRASSY FLATS by Penny Hayes. 256 pp. Lesbian romance in
the '30s.   ISBN 1-56280-010-8   9.95

A SINGULAR SPY by Amanda K. Williams. 192 pp. 3rd Madison
McGuire.   ISBN 1-56280-008-6   8.95

THE END OF APRIL by Penny Sumner. 240 pp. A Victoria Cross
Mystery. First in a series.   ISBN 1-56280-007-8   8.95

A FLIGHT OF ANGELS by Sarah Aldridge. 240 pp. Romance set at
the National Gallery of Art   ISBN 1-56280-001-9   9.95

HOUSTON TOWN by Deborah Powell. 208 pp. A Hollis Carpenter
mystery. Second in a series.   ISBN 1-56280-006-X   8.95

KISS AND TELL by Robbi Sommers. 192 pp. Scorching stories by
the author of *Pleasures*.   ISBN 1-56280-005-1   9.95

STILL WATERS by Pat Welch. 208 pp. A Helen Black mystery.
2nd in a series.   ISBN 0-941483-97-5   9.95

TO LOVE AGAIN by Evelyn Kennedy. 208 pp. Wildly
romantic love story.   ISBN 0-941483-85-1   9.95

IN THE GAME by Nikki Baker. 192 pp. A Virginia Kelly
mystery. First in a series.   ISBN 1-56280-004-3   9.95

AVALON by Mary Jane Jones. 256 pp. A Lesbian Arthurian
romance.   ISBN 0-941483-96-7   9.95

STRANDED by Camarin Grae. 320 pp. Entertaining, riveting
adventure.   ISBN 0-941483-99-1   9.95

THE DAUGHTERS OF ARTEMIS by Lauren Wright Douglas.
240 pp. A Caitlin Reece mystery. 3rd in a series.
                                               ISBN 0-941483-95-9   9.95

CLEARWATER by Catherine Ennis. 176 pp. Romantic secrets
of a small Louisiana town.   ISBN 0-941483-65-7   8.95

THE HALLELUJAH MURDERS by Dorothy Tell. 176 pp. A Poppy
Dillworth mystery. 2nd in a series.   ISBN 0-941483-88-6   8.95

ZETA BASE by Judith Alguire. 208 pp. Lesbian triangle
on a future Earth.   ISBN 0-941483-94-0   9.95

SECOND CHANCE by Jackie Calhoun. 256 pp. Contemporary
Lesbian lives and loves.   ISBN 0-941483-93-2   9.95

BENEDICTION by Diane Salvatore. 272 pp. Striking,
contemporary romantic novel.   ISBN 0-941483-90-8   9.95

CALLING RAIN by Karen Marie Christa Minns. 240 pp.
Spellbinding, erotic love story   ISBN 0-941483-87-8   9.95

BLACK IRIS by Jeane Harris. 192 pp. Caroline's hidden past . . .
                                               ISBN 0-941483-68-1   8.95

TOUCHWOOD by Karin Kallmaker. 240 pp. Loving, May/
December romance.   ISBN 0-941483-76-2   9.95

BAYOU CITY SECRETS by Deborah Powell. 224 pp. A Hollis
Carpenter mystery. First in a series.   ISBN 0-941483-91-6   9.95

COP OUT by Claire McNab. 208 pp. A Carol Ashton mystery.
4th in a series.   ISBN 0-941483-84-3   9.95

LODESTAR by Phyllis Horn. 224 pp. Romantic, fast-moving
adventure.   ISBN 0-941483-83-5   8.95

THE BEVERLY MALIBU by Katherine V. Forrest. 288 pp. A
Kate Delafield Mystery. 3rd in a series.   ISBN 0-941483-48-7   9.95

THAT OLD STUDEBAKER by Lee Lynch. 272 pp. Andy's affair
with Regina and her attachment to her beloved car.
                                               ISBN 0-941483-82-7   9.95

PASSION'S LEGACY by Lori Paige. 224 pp. Sarah is swept into
the arms of Augusta Pym in this delightful historical romance.
                                               ISBN 0-941483-81-9   8.95

THE PROVIDENCE FILE by Amanda Kyle Williams. 256 pp.
Second Madison McGuire   ISBN 0-941483-92-4   8.95

I LEFT MY HEART by Jaye Maiman. 320 pp. A Robin Miller
Mystery. First in a series.   ISBN 0-941483-72-X   9.95

THE PRICE OF SALT by Patricia Highsmith (writing as Claire
Morgan). 288 pp. Classic lesbian novel, first issued in 1952 . . .
acknowledged by its author under her own, very famous, name.
                                               ISBN 1-56280-003-5   9.95

SIDE BY SIDE by Isabel Miller. 256 pp. From beloved author of
Patience and Sarah.   ISBN 0-941483-77-0   9.95

STAYING POWER: LONG TERM LESBIAN COUPLES
by Susan E. Johnson. 352 pp. Joys of coupledom.
                                               ISBN 0-941-483-75-4   12.95

SLICK by Camarin Grae. 304 pp. Exotic, erotic adventure.
                                               ISBN 0-941483-74-6   9.95

NINTH LIFE by Lauren Wright Douglas. 256 pp. A Caitlin
Reece mystery. 2nd in a series.   ISBN 0-941483-50-9   8.95

PLAYERS by Robbi Sommers. 192 pp. Sizzling, erotic novel.
                                               ISBN 0-941483-73-8   9.95

MURDER AT RED ROOK RANCH by Dorothy Tell. 224 pp.
A Poppy Dillworth mystery. 1st in a series.   ISBN 0-941483-80-0   8.95

LESBIAN SURVIVAL MANUAL by Rhonda Dickson.
112 pp. Cartoons!   ISBN 0-941483-71-1   8.95

A ROOM FULL OF WOMEN by Elisabeth Nonas. 256 pp.
Contemporary Lesbian lives.   ISBN 0-941483-69-X   9.95

PRIORITIES by Lynda Lyons 288 pp. Science fiction with
a twist.   ISBN 0-941483-66-5   8.95

THEME FOR DIVERSE INSTRUMENTS by Jane Rule. 208
pp. Powerful romantic lesbian stories.   ISBN 0-941483-63-0   8.95

LESBIAN QUERIES by Hertz & Ertman. 112 pp. The questions
you were too embarrassed to ask.   ISBN 0-941483-67-3   8.95

CLUB 12 by Amanda Kyle Williams. 288 pp. Espionage thriller
featuring a lesbian agent!   ISBN 0-941483-64-9   8.95

DEATH DOWN UNDER by Claire McNab. 240 pp. A Carol
Ashton mystery. 3rd in a series.   ISBN 0-941483-39-8   9.95

MONTANA FEATHERS by Penny Hayes. 256 pp. Vivian and
Elizabeth find love in frontier Montana.   ISBN 0-941483-61-4   8.95

CHESAPEAKE PROJECT by Phyllis Horn. 304 pp. Jessie &
Meredith in perilous adventure.   ISBN 0-941483-58-4   8.95

LIFESTYLES by Jackie Calhoun. 224 pp. Contemporary Lesbian
lives and loves.   ISBN 0-941483-57-6   9.95

VIRAGO by Karen Marie Christa Minns. 208 pp. Darsen has
chosen Ginny.   ISBN 0-941483-56-8   8.95

WILDERNESS TREK by Dorothy Tell. 192 pp. Six women on
vacation learning "new" skills.   ISBN 0-941483-60-6   8.95

MURDER BY THE BOOK by Pat Welch. 256 pp. A Helen
Black Mystery. First in a series.   ISBN 0-941483-59-2   9.95

LESBIANS IN GERMANY by Lillian Faderman & B. Eriksson.
128 pp. Fiction, poetry, essays.   ISBN 0-941483-62-2   8.95

THERE'S SOMETHING I'VE BEEN MEANING TO TELL
YOU Ed. by Loralee MacPike. 288 pp. Gay men and lesbians
coming out to their children.   ISBN 0-941483-44-4   9.95

LIFTING BELLY by Gertrude Stein. Ed. by Rebecca Mark. 104
pp. Erotic poetry.   ISBN 0-941483-51-7   8.95

ROSE PENSKI by Roz Perry. 192 pp. Adult lovers in a long-term
relationship.   ISBN 0-941483-37-1   8.95

AFTER THE FIRE by Jane Rule. 256 pp. Warm, human novel
by this incomparable author.   ISBN 0-941483-45-2   8.95

SUE SLATE, PRIVATE EYE by Lee Lynch. 176 pp. The gay
folk of Peacock Alley are *all cats*.   ISBN 0-941483-52-5   8.95

CHRIS by Randy Salem. 224 pp. Golden oldie. Handsome Chris
and her adventures.   ISBN 0-941483-42-8   8.95

THREE WOMEN by March Hastings. 232 pp. Golden oldie. A
triangle among wealthy sophisticates.   ISBN 0-941483-43-6   8.95

RICE AND BEANS by Valeria Taylor. 232 pp. Love and
romance on poverty row.   ISBN 0-941483-41-X   8.95

PLEASURES by Robbi Sommers. 204 pp. Unprecedented
eroticism.   ISBN 0-941483-49-5   8.95

EDGEWISE by Camarin Grae. 372 pp. Spellbinding
adventure.   ISBN 0-941483-19-3   9.95

FATAL REUNION by Claire McNab. 224 pp. A Carol Ashton
mystery. 2nd in a series.   ISBN 0-941483-40-1   8.95

KEEP TO ME STRANGER by Sarah Aldridge. 372 pp. Romance
set in a department store dynasty.   ISBN 0-941483-38-X   9.95

IN THE BLOOD by Lauren Wright Douglas. 252 pp. Lesbian
science fiction adventure fantasy   ISBN 0-941483-22-3   8.95

THE BEE'S KISS by Shirley Verel. 216 pp. Delicate, delicious
romance.   ISBN 0-941483-36-3   8.95

RAGING MOTHER MOUNTAIN by Pat Emmerson. 264 pp.
Furosa Firechild's adventures in Wonderland.   ISBN 0-941483-35-5   8.95

IN EVERY PORT by Karin Kallmaker. 228 pp. Jessica's sexy,
adventuresome travels.   ISBN 0-941483-37-7   9.95

OF LOVE AND GLORY by Evelyn Kennedy. 192 pp. Exciting
WWII romance.   ISBN 0-941483-32-0   8.95

CLICKING STONES by Nancy Tyler Glenn. 288 pp. Love
transcending time.   ISBN 0-941483-31-2   9.95

SURVIVING SISTERS by Gail Pass. 252 pp. Powerful love
story.   ISBN 0-941483-16-9   8.95

SOUTH OF THE LINE by Catherine Ennis. 216 pp. Civil War
adventure.   ISBN 0-941483-29-0   8.95

WOMAN PLUS WOMAN by Dolores Klaich. 300 pp. Supurb
Lesbian overview.   ISBN 0-941483-28-2   9.95

HEAVY GILT by Delores Klaich. 192 pp. Lesbian detective/
disappearing homophobes/upper class gay society.

                                           ISBN 0-941483-25-8   8.95

THE FINER GRAIN by Denise Ohio. 216 pp. Brilliant young
college lesbian novel.   ISBN 0-941483-11-8   8.95

HIGH CONTRAST by Jessie Lattimore. 264 pp. Women of the
Crystal Palace.   ISBN 0-941483-17-7   8.95

OCTOBER OBSESSION by Meredith More. Josie's rich, secret
Lesbian life.   ISBN 0-941483-18-5   8.95

BEFORE STONEWALL: THE MAKING OF A GAY AND
LESBIAN COMMUNITY by Andrea Weiss & Greta Schiller.
96 pp., 25 illus.   ISBN 0-941483-20-7   7.95

WE WALK THE BACK OF THE TIGER by Patricia A. Murphy.
192 pp. Romantic Lesbian novel/beginning women's movement.
                                           ISBN 0-941483-13-4   8.95

SUNDAY'S CHILD by Joyce Bright. 216 pp. Lesbian athletics, at
last the novel about sports.   ISBN 0-941483-12-6   8.95

OSTEN'S BAY by Zenobia N. Vole. 204 pp. Sizzling adventure
romance set on Bonaire.   ISBN 0-941483-15-0   8.95

LESSONS IN MURDER by Claire McNab. 216 pp. A Carol
Ashton mystery. First in a series.   ISBN 0-941483-14-2   9.95

YELLOWTHROAT by Penny Hayes. 240 pp. Margarita, bandit,
kidnaps Julia.   ISBN 0-941483-10-X   8.95

SAPPHISTRY: THE BOOK OF LESBIAN SEXUALITY by
Pat Califia. 3d edition, revised. 208 pp.   ISBN 0-941483-24-X   10.95

CHERISHED LOVE by Evelyn Kennedy. 192 pp. Erotic
Lesbian love story.   ISBN 0-941483-08-8   9.95

LAST SEPTEMBER by Helen R. Hull. 208 pp. Six stories & a
glorious novella.   ISBN 0-941483-09-6   8.95

THE SECRET IN THE BIRD by Camarin Grae. 312 pp. Striking,
psychological suspense novel.   ISBN 0-941483-05-3   8.95

SURPLUS by Sylvia Stevenson. 342 pp. A classic early Lesbian
novel.   ISBN 0-930044-78-9   7.95

PEMBROKE PARK by Michelle Martin. 256 pp. Derring-do
and daring romance in Regency England.   ISBN 0-930044-77-0   7.95

THE LONG TRAIL by Penny Hayes. 248 pp. Vivid adventures
of two women in love in the old west.   ISBN 0-930044-76-2   8.95

AN EMERGENCE OF GREEN by Katherine V. Forrest. 288
pp. Powerful novel of sexual discovery.   ISBN 0-930044-69-X   9.95

THE LESBIAN PERIODICALS INDEX edited by Claire
Potter. 432 pp. Author & subject index.   ISBN 0-930044-74-6   12.95

DESERT OF THE HEART by Jane Rule. 224 pp. A classic;
basis for the movie *Desert Hearts*.   ISBN 0-930044-73-8   9.95

FOR KEEPS by Elisabeth Nonas. 144 pp. Contemporary novel
about losing and finding love.   ISBN 0-930044-71-1   7.95

TORCHLIGHT TO VALHALLA by Gale Wilhelm. 128 pp.
Classic novel by a great Lesbian writer. ISBN 0-930044-68-1   7.95

LESBIAN NUNS: BREAKING SILENCE edited by Rosemary
Curb and Nancy Manahan. 432 pp. Unprecedented autobiographies
of religious life.   ISBN 0-930044-62-2   9.95

THE SWASHBUCKLER by Lee Lynch. 288 pp. Colorful novel
set in Greenwich Village in the sixties. ISBN 0-930044-66-5   8.95

MISFORTUNE'S FRIEND by Sarah Aldridge. 320 pp. Historical Lesbian novel set on two continents. ISBN 0-930044-67-3   7.95

SEX VARIANT WOMEN IN LITERATURE by Jeannette
Howard Foster. 448 pp. Literary history. ISBN 0-930044-65-7   8.95

A HOT-EYED MODERATE by Jane Rule. 252 pp. Hard-hitting
essays on gay life; writing; art.   ISBN 0-930044-57-6   7.95

WE TOO ARE DRIFTING by Gale Wilhelm. 128 pp. Timeless
Lesbian novel, a masterpiece.   ISBN 0-930044-61-4   6.95

AMATEUR CITY by Katherine V. Forrest. 224 pp. A Kate
Delafield mystery. First in a series.   ISBN 0-930044-55-X   9.95

THE SOPHIE HOROWITZ STORY by Sarah Schulman. 176
pp. Engaging novel of madcap intrigue.   ISBN 0-930044-54-1   7.95

THE YOUNG IN ONE ANOTHER'S ARMS by Jane Rule.
224 pp. Classic Jane Rule.   ISBN 0-930044-53-3   9.95

OLD DYKE TALES by Lee Lynch. 224 pp. Extraordinary
stories of our diverse Lesbian lives.   ISBN 0-930044-51-7   8.95

DAUGHTERS OF A CORAL DAWN by Katherine V. Forrest.
240 pp. Novel set in a Lesbian new world. ISBN 0-930044-50-9   9.95

AGAINST THE SEASON by Jane Rule. 224 pp. Luminous,
complex novel of interrelationships.   ISBN 0-930044-48-7   8.95

LOVERS IN THE PRESENT AFTERNOON by Kathleen
Fleming. 288 pp. A novel about recovery and growth.
ISBN 0-930044-46-0   8.95

TOOTHPICK HOUSE by Lee Lynch. 264 pp. Love between
two Lesbians of different classes.   ISBN 0-930044-45-2   7.95

MADAME AURORA by Sarah Aldridge. 256 pp. Historical
novel featuring a charismatic ''seer.''   ISBN 0-930044-44-4   7.95

CONTRACT WITH THE WORLD by Jane Rule. 340 pp.
Powerful, panoramic novel of gay life.   ISBN 0-930044-28-2   9.95

THE NESTING PLACE by Sarah Aldridge. 224 pp. A
three-woman triangle — love conquers all!   ISBN 0-930044-26-6   7.95

THIS IS NOT FOR YOU by Jane Rule. 284 pp. A letter to a
beloved is also an intricate novel.   ISBN 0-930044-25-8   8.95

ANNA'S COUNTRY by Elizabeth Lang. 208 pp. A woman
finds her Lesbian identity.   ISBN 0-930044-19-3   8.95

PRISM by Valerie Taylor. 158 pp. A love affair between two
women in their sixties.   ISBN 0-930044-18-5   6.95

OUTLANDER by Jane Rule. 207 pp. Short stories and essays
by one of our finest writers.   ISBN 0-930044-17-7   8.95

ALL TRUE LOVERS by Sarah Aldridge. 292 pp. Romantic
novel set in the 1930s and 1940s.   ISBN 0-930044-10-X   8.95

CYTHEREA'S BREATH by Sarah Aldridge. 240 pp. Romantic
novel about women's entrance into medicine.
ISBN 0-930044-02-9   6.95

TOTTIE by Sarah Aldridge. 181 pp. Lesbian romance in the
turmoil of the sixties.   ISBN 0-930044-01-0   6.95

THE LATECOMER by Sarah Aldridge. 107 pp. A delicate love
story.   ISBN 0-930044-00-2   6.95

ODD GIRL OUT by Ann Bannon.   ISBN 0-930044-83-5   5.95
I AM A WOMAN 84-3; WOMEN IN THE SHADOWS 85-1;   each
JOURNEY TO A WOMAN 86-X; BEEBO BRINKER 87-8. Golden
oldies about life in Greenwich Village.

JOURNEY TO FULFILLMENT, A WORLD WITHOUT MEN, and   3.95
RETURN TO LESBOS. All by Valerie Taylor   each

These are just a few of the many Naiad Press titles — we are the oldest and
largest lesbian/feminist publishing company in the world. Please request a
complete catalog. We offer personal service; we encourage and welcome direct
mail orders from individuals who have limited access to bookstores carrying
our publications.